The Man Who Spoiled the Music

Also from Westphalia Press
westphaliapress.org

The Man Who Spoiled the Music

and Other Stories

by Mark Guy Pearse

WESTPHALIA PRESS
An imprint of Policy Studies Organization

Westphalia Press
An imprint of Policy Studies Organization
1527 New Hampshire Ave., NW
Washington, D.C. 20036
info@ipsonet.org

ISBN-13: 978-1-63391-392-9
ISBN-10: 1-63391-392-9

Cover design by Taillefer Long at Illuminated Stories:
www.illuminatedstories.com

Daniel Gutierrez-Sandoval, Executive Director
PSO and Westphalia Press

Updated material and comments on this edition
can be found at the Westphalia Press website:
www.westphaliapress.org

THE MAN WHO SPOILED
THE MUSIC

AND OTHER STORIES

BY

MARK GUY PEARSE

AUTHOR OF "DANIEL QUORM AND HIS RELIGIOUS NOTIONS,"
"THOUGHTS ON HOLINESS," ETC., ETC.

ILLUSTRATED BY CHARLES TRESIDDER

LONDON
CHARLES H. KELLY, 2, CASTLE ST., CITY RD., E.C.
AND 66, PATERNOSTER ROW, E.C.
1892

It was the dinner hour and they sat together in the sunshine.

[*Page* 167.

CONTENTS.

LIST OF ILLUSTRATIONS.

The Man who Spoiled the Music.

THERE was no doubt about it—*he did*. The faintest shadow of a doubt was gone. *He was the man who spoiled the music.*

And yet it was the last thing that he was likely to believe. He loved music. His voice was often

heard ringing out a rollicking song in the tap-
room, swelling above all the rest as they joined
in the chorus, holding the unsteady voices together,
in a way that indicated much force and not a little
skill. And yet he spoiled all the music! It was
most certainly so. The more he turned it over the
more he saw it. It was no good arguing; no good
denying it. He might get as angry as he liked,
there was the fact all the same. *He was the man who
spoiled the music.*

It was a discovery that came as a great shock to
him; for he had always been the first to drop upon
anybody else who got out of tune. The slightest
tendency astray to sharp or flat, to fast or slow, was
sure to rouse his anger, and all were pulled up with
much ado that he might correct the offender. And
now to think that it should keep coming to him in
at least a score of different ways—he himself was the
man who spoiled the music!

He was not in the brightest possible condition for
an argument, and certainly not in a humour to be
convinced of a truth that he did not want to believe;
and yet convinced he was, and every minute added to
the conviction. Every sight about him, and the
silence, if not the sounds, forced it home upon him,
so that there could not possibly be any mistake.

It was Sunday afternoon, about four o'clock. He
was standing leaning against the wall by the dirty

fireplace, unwashed, and in his shirt-sleeves, with hands thrust deep into his pockets, and the great un-laced boots thrust far out on the floor. The dull eyes, the knitted brows, the mouth drawn sourly down at the corners, completed a picture of misery. The room looked as wretched as the man himself, and as dirty; blackened and broken, with window-panes either plastered over with paper or stuffed out with rags. The rickety furniture was there simply because it could fetch nothing elsewhere. Seated on the other side of the fireplace was the white-faced and slatternly wife, holding a tiny bit of mortality at her breast, and breathing a heavy sigh that told of a burden there a great deal heavier than the baby.

One word summed up the whole reason of the wretchedness—*Drink*. Not a bad sort of a man but for this one thing; able to earn good wages and to have a comfortable home, yet no idle miscreant ever dwelt amidst greater squalor, or kept all about him in greater misery. What was he the better for brains that had been the pride of his old mother, and which fitted him to get on as well as anybody and better than most, so long as drink kept him on a level with the biggest numskulls of the parish? What was he the better for being a clever workman and earning good wages, whilst drink made his pocket as empty, his family as starved, his home as wretched as if he had neither a straight eye nor a clever hand? And worse than that—many a bitter grief would never have been known there if that had been all. Poverty does not bring the heaviest or worst burden folks have to carry in God's world. The woman, who once found in him her joy, now sitting a broken-hearted wife; the home with its dainty bits of furniture, and all about it so bright and clean, gone for this; the children often wanting clothes and bread, yet dreading no want so much as they dreaded their father's presence: it was only the curse of drunkenness that could work such mischief.

So it came about that on this Sunday afternoon Jack stood as cross as cross could be, ready to let out his misery upon the first victim he could find, as if anyone were to be blamed for it sooner than himself. Then it was that the door opened suddenly with a bang, and in burst two little maidens singing merrily: eyes and faces, hands and feet, all were full of music. They had come from the Mission Sunday-school, and the last hymn was in their ears, and came cheerily ringing from their lips—

> "I am so glad that our Father in heaven
> Tells of His love in the Book He has given."

They had just got to the line of the chorus: "I am so glad," and it came in at the opened door with such a bounding gladness as they lifted the latch and felt that they were in the freedom of the home—"I am so glad—" then suddenly they came far enough to see their father. Instantly the voices were silenced, the sunshine died out of their eyes; with a frightened look filling their faces they shrank outside the door again, and shut it noiselessly.

The silence that followed was unbroken by a sound. The wife sat mournfully looking at the blackened ashes of the fireplace, with the little one asleep in her arms. That abrupt and sudden silence smote Jack's heart; those changed faces, and the little frightened maidens hushed like that—he felt that he had done it all. He seemed to hear again the happy burst—"I am so glad"—and then that dreadful stopping. He was going to ask with an oath why they didn't go on singing, but they weren't there, and so it was no use to do that; besides, he knew well enough, too well, why they had stopped; so it came about that he lifted himself from the wall and thrust himself fiercely into his jacket, and went slouching towards the door. He strode out of the court and away on, anywhere, until he got outside the streets and into the more quiet and pleasant roads; then he slackened his pace. The fierceness had turned to grief, and at last there came the words muttered to himself: "*That's what I am always doing—I spoil all the music.*"

Now when once he admitted the truth to himself, there stood, as we have intimated, at least a hundred

witnesses that took up the matter and confirmed it
in many ways, until Jack was ready to declare with
an oath that he didn't do anything of the sort, and
that they had better not repeat the statement.　But
then no sooner were all these witnesses driven out of
court, than again he heard those bright little voices,
and again he saw their sunny faces, and again there
came the burst of singing: "I am so glad"—and
then there came again that dreadful silence and fear;
and immediately the evidence rose up and clamoured
against him more loudly than ever.　So it went on
until at last poor Jack gave right in and just let
them go on as they would.

"*Yes, 'tis true, I spoil all the music,*" said Jack.

And the more he thought of it the worse it grew,
until it spread itself in all directions.　Slowly and
one after another, came the long procession of witnesses, who pointed at him and gave their evidence
against him. as the man who spoiled their music.
The first was enough if there had been no other.　It
was the dear old mother who had toiled and scraped
and saved for him, her only son, and so proud of him
as she was, too.　And he remembered how proudly
he used to think that in her old age he would keep
the roof over her head, and make her glad for all that
she had done.　And she, needing many a comfort
that he could have given her, had gone down sorrowing over him to her grave.　An old saint, she had

learned the new song in heaven, but it was little comfort to think that but for him she might have been singing still upon earth.

" *I spoiled her music*," Jack sighed very sadly.

Then there came the poor wife, so white-faced and wretched, with that little bit of a baby at her breast. Away behind her, ever so far, Jack saw other times when they had sung together. What a sweet voice she had then! He could hear it still as she kept singing about the farmhouse all day long. He could hear it again, when it seemed best of all, on the still summer evening as she came home from milking. How often his path used to lie that way, and what happy days they were, she with the bright face and the roses in it a deeper red for his coming. And now to think of her sitting there in that miserable room, so white and still. She never sang the baby off to sleep now. "Anyhow, not when I am there," Jack sighed again; " *I spoil all the music*."

Then out of the past there came another Jack— a decent fellow who wouldn't have looked at this dirty and ragged lounger; a man with his head up and a cheery voice that rang out in the lanes as he went to work in the early morning, and that kept time with the plane as he sent the shavings flying from the bench ; who whistled the tune as he held up the bit of work and let his eye run along it to see if it were true, taking a pride in it, and then

singing on again. And on Sundays—no wonder
poor Jack sighed again—it was hard to believe that
it was he who sang in the choir and used to take
such a delight in it all.

"*I spoil all the music,*" said Jack again, "*everywhere.*" And at every pause and interval there
came again the sight of those merry faces darkened,
and those glad voices silenced at the sight of him.
" And I their own father," sighed Jack again ; " poor
little dears, to go spoiling *their* music, too ! "

Jack's trouble seemed to grow bigger every
minute, until at last things began to get desperate.
Dark and awful temptations flew about him. He
would end it all; the wife and little ones couldn't
be worse off than they were, and he, at any rate,
would not be spoiling other people's music when he
was dead. But before the grim thought had well
got hold of him, he seemed to see again the
sunny faces, and to hear the merry voices singing
their song : " I am so glad." And with the thought
of them this time there came a softer feeling and
a gentler tone. " Poor little things," he sighed
again ; " it wouldn't mend their music either if I
was gone. Nor hers either," he said to himself a
little while afterwards, as he thought of the white-
faced wife and the little bit of mortality at home
there.

So it came about that poor Jack, so burdened and

helpless, stopped there and then and put his face into his hands and said: " God help me." He had gone on, never thinking where he was going, until now he found himself outside the long stretch of the houses, and was under the green trees, and in the midst of the fields. The lark sang overhead, the thrush and the blackbird rang out their richest notes; in the branches above him a crowd of sparrows met and chirped the very loudest, merriest music they had ever learnt.

He stood leaning on a gate while the sunset fell full upon him. His hands hung over the bar, and the tears glistened in the ruddy glow of the setting sun. Was there any help for him? Down so low, could he ever get up again? All about him was calm and still and beautiful, and seemed to condemn him as he stood there, so ragged and wretched, making such misery in the world. He looked away to the setting sun. "If I could only get right off and begin again," he sighed; "right out of the reach of the old ways." But this seemed only to mock him. " Begin again," he muttered, grimly; " I have got nothing to begin on ! "

For a while despair came on him once more. It was no use his trying, not a bit. He must just go on to the end.

So, burdened and sorrowing, Jack leaned still over the gate. He had given up thinking, and now just let the thoughts come and go, scarcely heeding them. The sun had set. The music of the birds was hushed. Here and there a silver star shone overhead. Then it was that once more Jack seemed to hear the two little voices and their glad song—

> " I am so glad that our Father in heaven
> Tells of His love in the Book He has given."

The words sang themselves over and over again in his soul, soothing by the flow of the words rather than by their meaning. They lulled to sleep the fierce feelings that had filled him.

But as the words went sinking down within him, they began to speak to his heart.

" Our Father in heaven," he whispered, and there came back the story of one who had wasted his substance in riotous living; and how he arose and came to his father, and how, when he was yet a great way off, his father saw him, and ran and fell upon his neck and kissed him, and put about him the best robe and the ring on his finger and the shoes on his feet. " But then," Jack sighed again, and shook his head sadly, " he only spoiled his own music—I've spoiled so many other people's."

But still the voices sang on in his soul—

> "I am so glad that our Father in heaven
> Tells of His love in the Book He has given."

As they sang on they seemed to gather strength

until his heart heard them again, and took hold of
them once more. " Our Father in heaven," he
whispered, and there came distinct and living the
memory of how he had kneeled long ago at his
mother's knee ; he felt again that gentle hand laid
upon his head, and heard that voice teaching him
the words—" Our Father Who art in heaven."
Might he not say those words ?   Ah, if he could only
go back again, and be the little child at the mother's
knee !

Then Jack buried his face in his hands and just
let his heart flow out with the words of the
Lord's Prayer.   Slowly he went through the petitions
until he reached the last.   THINE IS THE KINGDOM,
AND THE POWER, AND THE GLORY, FOR EVER AND
EVER.   He stopped, and spoke them over to himself slowly three or four times.   Then his soul took
hold of them.   They came as new life to a dying man.
Here was all he needed—if he got that help he need
fear nothing—companions, habits, anything, anybody—what were all these if only this Power was on
his side.   And it was ; he knew it ; he was sure of
it.   " Thine *is* the Kingdom and the Power and the
Glory—what for ? " he asked himself, with all the
fierceness turned now into a defiant triumph.   Not
only to set stars in the heavens, and to make glorious
sunsets, and to grow great trees ; and to let a man
go down all helpless to hell !   "Thine *is* the Kingdom

and the Power." Then surely it was on purpose for
such as he was.

As for love, the poor fellow found himself utterly
unworthy of that; it did not come anywhere within
the range of his hopes. But a father who was as
strong as "our Father in heaven," would help a man
though he might not be able to love him. "Thine
is the Kingdom and the Power," said Jack, as he
lifted himself up from the gate, and he laid hold of
the truth like a sword, with which he could defy all
enemies. "I don't want to get away now," he said,
and he longed that he could go right there and then
and fight the drink and all its surroundings.

It was quite dark as he passed into the squalid
court in which he lived. He turned into the wretched
house; but he could look at it all now without fear.
It should all come right. "Thine is the Kingdom and
the Power," said Jack, and he said it with a feeling
like that with which a soldier grips his sword at the
footstep of an enemy.

The next day he was up and off at daylight.
Vexed and desperate as he was, he went at his work
with a grim fierceness, without a word for anybody.
His mates were used to his moods, and did not care
to interfere with him at times like these. "Jack is
out again about some'at," said they, with a jerk of the
thumb in his direction. They might stop for dinner,
but Jack snatched at a bit of bread and worked on;

they might pack up at the stroke of the clock, but so long as the light lasted Jack would stick to it. "This is not spoiling anybody's music, anyhow," said he fiercely to one man who ventured to hint that he had done enough for that day. He came home and sat at his supper, with wife and children creeping noiselessly and frightened about the house. Poor Jack! a tear came gathering in the corner of his eye and fell down his cheek. "I do wish they'd sing a bit, but I expect I've spoiled all the music for ever," he muttered to himself. He longed to get them about him, wife and little ones, and to take the sleeping babe from its poor little rags, and to tell them all that was in his heart; but somehow he couldn't manage it, and so he just crept off to bed.

"Not yet," he muttered, "but some time soon, by God's help. Thine *is* the Kingdom and the Power."

Jack's fit was on the next day, much to the surprise of his mates; the brow knit and the lips tight, and the work flying on at a tremendous pace. "Why, Jack, lad," cried one, "art thou putting a week o' work into a day, that thou mayst go on spree all the rest of it?"

"No," said Jack so gruffly that nobody had a word for him again; and so it lasted, Wednesday, Thursday, Friday. All that was strange enough, and set his workmates wondering; but strangest of all was it when that Saturday afternoon came, and

Jack took up his wages without a word and just walked right away from them all, and home. " Jack's mad," said they. " Never knew his fit last so long as this."

" Now," said Jack, taking a stride just double the usual length, and putting his foot down as if he meant to get through to the other side of the earth, " I'll try and get the music back again," and Jack meant to smile, but he had to put his mouth tight and to knit his brows to keep back a tear. " By God's help," Jack added, devoutly.

When he came home he evidently was not expected ; indeed, was scarcely wanted. There was not very much to be tidied up, and his wife, poor thing ! had not much heart to do that little. But much or little, she was now in the middle of the process, and so the " bits of sticks," as they were called, were put on one side whilst the good wife kneeled and scrubbed away at the floor with the handle of a brush on which a few straggling hairs remained as if to keep up the name. The wife lifted her face in surprise, and then just went on again with her scrubbing. Whatever this coming home meant, nothing ever brought her any good.

Poor Jack, he seemed to hear it all. " Spoilt her music too," he sighed. He hung up his bag of tools on the peg, and took off the apron that was rolled about his waist ; and then he caught sight of that venerable and hairless scrubbing brush. " It will help to bring back the music," said Jack to himself, purposing to buy his wife there and then a new one. But the purpose was somewhat delayed. Just then, from some corner of the room there came the cry of the baby. The wife was rising up to get at it when Jack dived in after the little bundle of rags and fetched it out.

" I'll hold her a bit," said Jack, rather shyly.

Jack's wife would like to have said " Thank you," but she felt shy too.

" Now, Jack, try and mend the music," said he to himself, and this time he really did smile ; for the baby was unused to strangers, and none was a greater stranger to it than its own father, so it just cried out lustily. The good wife scrubbed on. There were times when she had to let it cry a bit, and this should be one of them. Jack took the little one tenderly into his arms and leaned against the wall. He put his lips tightly together and chirped to it—just a tiny little chirp like a young sparrow having its first music lesson. But the baby cried louder than ever. Then Jack put forth his strength and chirped to it louder and faster. Not a bit of use was that ; still it cried. It was wonderful how such a poor little wizened frame could make such a noise. Then Jack put the baby on the other arm and set his tongue against his teeth and clicked to it. " Click, click, click," went

Jack, quite loud enough to start a good coach-and-four. Bless you, he might as well have winked at the baby. Jack changed sides again, and then he whistled. Now, Jack prided himself on his whistling. He might not be much of a hand at chirping, and at clicking he was willing to give in. But as for whistling, Jack *could* whistle, and so he whistled shrill and loud, fast and wild, a whistle loud enough for a drum and fife band, and fast enough for the wildest Irish jig. But the baby cried on just as loud as ever.

Jack was in no humour to give in; the spirit of grim defiance with which he had met everything about him through all the week could not afford to be conquered by a little thing like this. Jack took it up in his hands and held the baby aloft and danced it to and fro. But still the baby cried.

The good wife rose from her scrubbing and began to wipe her hands in the apron; she must take it.

But Jack would try once more; it really was not pleasant to be beaten like this. So, setting himself resolutely against the wall, Jack began to sing.

At first it was soft and low, like a man who was feeling his way. But gathering courage as he went, presently he was rolling out an old song of long ago with all the force of his voice.

The effect was magical. The baby stopped as if it were charmed. It opened its eyes to their widest. Then it opened its mouth in imitation of the father's. It put out tiny hands and laid hold firmly of his whiskers as if it would keep him at it. Then it laughed and crowed with delight.

"Eh, Jack, it is good to hear thy music again," his wife said, very quietly.

Poor Jack, it almost put him out. He did stop for a moment, but instantly the little face puckered and wrinkled into all sorts of lines; the eyes closed, the nose was squeezed together, and the lips began to quiver with the coming cry. Then Jack had to strike off again, only to find the effect as magical as before, and to hear the baby laughing and crowing once more; and in the midst of it all there came in the two little maidens, to find the father leaning against the wall making music like this.

"Why, we couldn't think whoever it was, father," said they, wondering, and without the merriment fading from their eyes this time.

They sat at tea, silent and shy, every one of them wondering except the baby; that kept stretching out its arms to the father, and found a new delight in pulling at his whiskers.

Poor Jack, he wanted all his thoughts about him to say what he found it so hard to say, but words wouldn't come; and the most eloquent would find it hard to talk when a tiny hand was being thrust in one's mouth, and another tugged at the beard. So Jack had to content himself with putting his hand

C

into his pocket, and taking out one sovereign and one half sovereign and gave them to his wife.

"What's this, Jack?" she asked, going to the window, for it was getting darkish, and she feared the first glance had deceived her.

"Wages," said Jack, getting it out as well as he could.

The poor wife looked at the money, and then she looked at him. She bit each of the coins, and then looked as if she would like to apply at least her lips to Jack's. But she put the money in her pocket, or rather we should have said, pockets, for Jack's wife had two. One of them was a very easily reached affair; there, in the thin and tattered dress that she wore, you could not help seeing its somewhat obtrusive opening, for long use had kept its mouth widely agape. Into this went common things of all kinds, for which no other resting place might be handy, and its contents bulged prominently as the good wife moved about the house. But the other—where it was, it is not for us to know; away and underneath somewhere, to get at it involving much turning and searching. Here, alas! was the only safe place for the little that the good wife could scrape together to put by for the children's shoes and such occasional expenditure. And not always sacred here in these depths; the hard earned little bits of silver would sometimes have to go in a scrap of meat for Sunday's dinner, and even for a loaf of bread. Now, it was within and away in the more secret pocket that she had put the sovereign, that might, perhaps, be hers. But the half-sovereign was in the outer common pocket. Jack would be sure to want that before long, and it should be ready for him, since he had trusted her like this, and she felt that if this kind of thing went on she would have to sing too.

" I'll stay and take care of the little ones, if you want to go out, wife," said Jack. True, it was spoken with some interruption, and more than one word was bobbed back into his mouth by that little hand; but it went down into the good wife's heart, and stirred music that she had not heard for many a long day.

" Bless thee, lad! it is good of thee," said the wife, and then she blushed like a maiden that she should have said so much.

" 'Tis all thine, wife, so don't be afraid," said Jack, as the wife went out at the door.

She turned back with a great stare. " All this," said she; " Why, Jack! what must I do with it?"

" Buy thyself a new scrubbing brush, and get the baby a new frock for Sunday," and this time Jack did smile.

The wife came nearer; she couldn't help it; she stood for a moment plucking up courage, then she put her hand on his shoulder, and stooped down and kissed the baby, and took a long time over it, too.

" I should like to give thee one, too," she said, as shyly as possible ; and she did it splendidly, and then hurried away.

" I think the music is coming back again," said Jack to himself.

.   .   .   .

Later that night, after his wife came back, Jack went marketing, and a couple of chairs were set by the fire.   " Good kind of musical boxes," said Jack to himself, as he took them in at the door and set each in its place.   And there, about the fire, they sat side by side, silent for a while, the baby asleep, and the little maidens at his side.

" Come, little ones, you must sing to mother and me," said he, at last.   " ' I am so glad,' you know."

And they looked at each other with a wonder that soon passed into sunshine and joy ; and before they knew it, Jack and his wife joined with them.   But poor Jack broke down before he had gone on long ; then the others broke down, too, and all was still for a while, until Jack wiped away his tears and looked up cheerily.

" Eh, but I mustn't spoil the music like this ; sing on, little ones ; " and they did sing, and Jack sang, and his wife.   And then Jack did as he hadn't done for many a day ; he knelt down with wife and children, and asked God to help them and bless them, to forgive the past, and to strengthen him for the future.

On the Sunday, there they sat together at the little Mission room, and from that day to this, no voice is clearer or louder than Jack's. And now, whenever he talks about clumsy work, or faults in anything, Jack always calls it " *Spoiling the music.*"

Jack soon found out that the power that helped him thus, was the power of God's great love; and the grim spirit gave place to gentleness. It was some weeks afterwards that one night in the Mission room Jack stood up to say a few words.

" I can sing, mates, better than I can talk; but I should be ashamed if I could not tell you something about what ' Our Father in heaven ' has done for me. I used to think that religion was no good but to die with. There never was a bigger mistake than that. I find it just the grandest thing that ever was for to live with. Talking about going to heaven when you die—why, when Christ was born didn't heaven come down to earth ? And I believe that wherever Christ comes, He brings heaven with Him, if we'll only open the door wide enough. Ask the wife here, she knows if I am speaking truth or no. Ask the little ones here. Why bless you, that there baby, though it ain't more than a few months old, is old enough to know the difference."

Then Jack's eyes filled with tears, and he found it rather hard work to get on.

" Bless ye, lads, my heart is a-singing, though my eyes be a bit waterish, but it is only the joy running over. I tell ye, it's enough to keep a man singing all the day long, and sometimes it's more than you can let out with your tongue. I know now, mates, what the blessed Lord Jesus Christ came into the world for, and what He died for, and what He is living to do for us every one, and I do bless Him for it. 'Tis that He may bring back the music, and keep us from spoiling it."

Then Jack's voice got a bit husky again.

"I used to go boozing and soaking in the public-house every night, and here was the dear missis crying her eyes out, and a-breaking her heart about it. Here was the little ones ragged and almost barefoot, afraid of their father's footstep more than of anything else in the world. Here was the house stripped bare of everything comfortable and decent ; and here was me, a plague and a nuisance to everybody. That *was* spoiling the music, if you like. But now, lads, I should like you to hear the concerts and lovely tunes I've got now all day long. Bless ye, there's no need to pay a big price for a ticket, you can have it very cheap, and it's a sort of music that don't get hoarse in damp weather. To go home when the work's done and see the light dancing in the little ones' eyes because father's come ; to find the wife looking happy enough for a princess, and to hear the baby laugh for joy,—ah, that's music that the angels in heaven might envy. To get about the fire and sing a hymn together, with the kettle a-keeping time, and then to read a chapter out of the blessed Book, and to kneel down and get a fresh stock of God's love in the heart, that's something like music. Then to go out to your work along with the blessed Lord Jesus —why, I reckon He was a carpenter on purpose to teach us that He had come to help us to do our work as well as ever it could be done. To have a clear eye and a steady hand, and a throat that isn't all parched up with the drink ; to find your work going like a merry tune of music all day long ; and to feel that you can keep a clean tongue in your head, and be patient with them that make a bit of mistake, and that you want to help everybody else a bit because the blessed Lord has helped you so much. What do ye call that, lads ? That's what I call music ! and thank God, that is what the Lord has done for me."

Jack's prayer every morning is : " *Lord, keep us in tune all day long.*" A prayer that has been blessedly answered now for many months.

"It won't Sink."

SOME years ago, when I was living on the east coast of England, I often used to go to sea for a night's trawling.

My companion on such occasions was a brave fisherman, himself at once the captain and crew of his craft. Though still a young man when he decided to be a soldier and servant of the Lord Jesus, yet his early life had been a somewhat wild one; and his career on board a ship that had regularly been engaged in smuggling, had given him many adventures of peril and daring. As for our craft, she was not much to look at: used chiefly for dredging the stones from which the " Roman " cement is prepared, she carried the marks of her hard service; but she had one quality that covered many defects, she could stand any amount of sea, as my friend had often proved—and I, too, sometimes, in the fierce easterly gales that broke upon that coast. With a fireplace for cooking, and a snug cabin for sleeping in, the roughness of it all rather added to the enjoyment.

But it was the company of my fisherman friend that was the special charm of these nights at sea. Simple and God-fearing, a quiet happiness seemed always singing in his soul that often broke out into some glad song of praise together as we drifted in the still evening, or flew before a stiff breeze. A man, too, who thought much, and had little opportunity of talking, so that I got from him many an opinion about things in general that it was good to hear.

It was as we sat together at daybreak, on a lovely morning in June, that he told me this story. We were drifting quietly along with the trawl overboard; not a sound was there to break the perfect stillness, except only the lapping of the water against the boat. Here and there shone the white sails of some ship, or floated the long line of smoke from some steamer. Behind us slept the country, with wooded hills and sloping corn-fields, and a house whose windows dazzled in the rays of the rising sun. All above us and about us stretched the wondrous beauty of the sky—the deep blue coming down to the green hills and the red cliffs; overhead there were the rosy hues, long lines of fleecy clouds growing more and more golden as they neared the water's edge, with straight lines of white light shooting up between them in singular regularity. Right in front of us went a broad sheet of pure gold, that led away to the sun as it was coming up out of the sea. A flock of gulls completed

the beauty and peacefulness of the scene—the " birds
of calm sat brooding on the charmed wave." Hushed,
and almost awed by the loveliness and sacredness of
it all, it seemed to us like a glimpse of some better
world, untouched by earth's defilement, undisturbed
by earth's ado—a world that belonged to God rather
than to man.

The deep feelings that were stirred within us
seemed to find their natural outlet, as we joined together in singing the morning hymn—

> " Awake, my soul, and with the sun
> Thy daily stage of duty run;
> Shake off dull sloth and joyful rise
> To pay thy morning sacrifice.
>   *   *   *
> Wake, and lift up thyself, my heart,
> And with the angels bear thy part,
> Who all night long unwearied sing
> High praise to the eternal King."

Our singing had ceased, and all was still again.
Presently my friend began :—" Ah, sir, this is very
different from what it used to be in the old time.
We never used to think much about the beauty of
the sea or the sky when day broke—nor about God
either. We should get out the telescope, and sweep
the sea all round to find if the Government cutter
was in sight, and only wished that the darkness had
lasted an hour or two longer, that we might have
got our cargo ashore.

" I can remember once "— and he laughed as he

spoke—" though, there—it was no laughing matter
then, at any rate for us. There was one morning
when we caught sight of her—far off, almost, as you
could see, but for all that we knew her rig in a
minute, and terribly put about we were, too—for we
had a full cargo aboard. At first we hoped that she
wasn't after us—or tried to, anyhow. But very soon
all hope was gone. She was bearing down upon us,
sir, as straight as a line.

" Of course, we knew that we could never get away
from her, do what we might. We looked at each
other, for every man knew well enough that if we were
caught, it meant prison for us —and it meant the loss
of the cargo, and ship, too—sawn in two, right
across : that was her punishment, in those times.
We were still enough for a minute or so, all of us
waiting for the captain to speak, and there all the
time that speck of a sail coming straight for us. It
was plain enough what she was bound for, and gain-
ing upon us, too.

" Presently he spoke out, ' Well, lads, there's no
help for it that I can see, but this—*let them come and
find a clear hold and an empty ship.* They may
make of it what they can, then. A man can't swing
for that, anyhow.'

" Well, sir, at it we went. We put a sail over the
side of the ship for a blind, and then to work. It
was tobacco, done up in canvas bags, made handy

for the sake of easy carrying. Half of us went down
in the hold, and flung up the bags as fast as ever we
could; and the rest were slipping them over the side
of the ship, under the sail and into the sea. Eh,
how we worked! 'Heave away, lads,' the captain
kept saying; 'as well not do it at all as leave a bag
behind—a single one will show them the game we've
been up to.'

"Bit by bit we were stripped to the waist, and
steaming with the heat of it, from captain to cabin-
boy. Pity enough it seemed, to be flinging the stuff
over like that; but it was too late to think about
that now. 'At it, my hearties,' says the captain.
'It will be something to laugh at to see the officer
come aboard, and set his chaps to search the ship,
and find an empty hold. Heave away, my lads.'

"We laughed at the captain's joke, and worked
all the fiercer for his bit of fun. Of course, the hold
soon began to show the difference in the cargo, working as we were. But we were beginning to get a bit
fagged and spent.

"'Fling away, lads,' the captain kept saying,
himself doing the work of two men. 'They will
spoil our laughing if they find anything left.'

"And then again it was still, except for the splash-
ing of the bags in the sea.

"We were beginning to think that we should do
it.

" ' A quarter of an hour more, and 'tis clear,' cried the captain, joyfully ; and every man felt as if he could breathe again. We were going at it for our lives, and never an eye or an ear for anything else. Presently the captain sees that the boy was getting a bit done up, and he tells him to run out and look how the cutter was coming along. He was gone for a second, and then he come back, and you wouldn't have known him. We all stopped to look at him— we couldn't help it. His face was as white as death ; and there he stood, with his eyes staring as if they would drop out of his head. His mouth was wide open, but he couldn't say a word, and his hands were stretched out before him. The captain began swearing at him, and asked him what he meant. But the lad, he couldn't utter a sound. It was more like a boy out of his senses than anything else. Then the captain jumps up, and grips his arm and shakes him. The poor little fellow managed to gasp out— ' *It won't sink !* ' and he fell down in a faint.

" ' *It won't sink !* ' We guessed in a moment what he meant. We hurried away to the stern of the ship, but nobody expected to see anything like the sight that was waiting for us there—a sight, sir, to fetch a man's heart out of him. It was a beautiful morning, like this. And there, right away in the glistening track of the sun, was the cargo. You could see the line of the canvas bags, rising with the bit of

swell, and shining in the light, one after the other
reaching away to the cutter herself; there they were,
every one of them proclaiming our guilt to all the
heaven above us, and to every ship that was up and
down the coast.   Our hands just sank to our side, and
there we sat, every man of us still as death, with his
eyes set on that dreadful line of evidence against us,
and every man with those words ringing in his soul
—' IT WON'T SINK ! ' "

  *   *   *   *   *

My friend was silent for a minute or two, and I
thought the story was finished, at anyrate so far as
he cared to tell it.   I had turned to enjoy the
delicious stillness and the exquisite beauty of the
scene, when he began again, but in another tone,—

" Well, sir, it did not end there.   I little thought
at the time what would come out of that empty hold;
and least of all that it could ever be any good.   Of
course, I often used to think a bit seriously about
things, and meant to mend ; but somehow it never
came to anything.   Still, my dear old mother kept
on praying for me, and in spite of everything she
would always hold to it that I should come right
some day.   ' Prayer is not much good if it isn't
stronger than the devil and sin,' she would say, even
when father and the rest of them had given me up.
It was somewhere about two or three years after the
adventure with the cutter, that one night—the last

night of the year, it was—I had gone down the river
in my boat, thinking I might get some wild fowl, for
there were a good many in the river. It was a dull,
misty night when I started. I got down some distance, and then pushed away in under the bank,
waiting for the moon to get up. It was all as still
and quiet as could be, with never a sound but now
and then the cry of a curlew, or the wings of the wild
ducks overhead. The moon was getting up behind
the hill, and the trees were standing all black against
the light, and the silver shining between their trunks
and branches. From ever so far off there came the
sound of a peal of bells, ringing the old year out.

" ' The last night of the year,' I said to myself.
Of course, I couldn't help feeling a bit sad at the
words, though I can hardly tell why. But as I sat
there in the stillness, it began to come to my mind
how I used to kneel down at my mother's side while
she taught me to pray. I could hear her voice quite
plain telling me of one good man and another, and of
what they had done to make the world better. And
I felt her hand laid upon my head again, and could
see her sitting by the fire with her eyes closed and
her lips moving, and I knew she was praying God to
bless me.

"I sighed as I thought of it all, and said half
aloud, 'If I died to-night, there isn't a soul in the
world that would thank God that I ever lived.' I

began to feel as if out of joint with everything. The
more I thought of it, the plainer I saw that my whole
life was a failure. God had made me for Himself,
and here I was living as if there was no God, and no
eternity. There would be a terrible account to
settle some day. And here, another year was almost
gone !

" I did not think myself any very great sinner—
not then—for I never got drunk, nor went into bad
ways like other fellows did. As for smuggling, it
never occurred to me that there was any harm in
that, except for the company it brought me into. It
was the emptiness and uselessness of my life that
kept troubling me. The moon was rising higher,
and the light fell on the flat stretch of shore opposite
to me ; gleaming in the pools here and there, and in
the little curves and hollows that the tide had left.
And somehow it came to be a picture of my life—it
lay ugly and useless like the mud, no good, you
couldn't grow anything in it, couldn't even walk on
it or build on it ! there was no foundation for anything. ' A life like that mudbank,' I said to myself,
with a shudder. My sad thoughts went slowly sinking down within me, until now the moon rose clear
and full in the sky, lighting up all the woods opposite to me, and seeming to make it stiller than
ever. Then out upon the silence came the pealing
of the bells. Should the new year be no better than

The poor little fellow managed to gasp out – ' It won't sink.'

the rest?—only another stretch of mud, foul and ugly and useless?

"I bowed my head on the side of the boat, and prayed God to help me. By His grace, from that night I would be another man. I would just give up anything, everything I could think of that hindered my being a good man. Though I did not get drunk, I made up my mind to have done with the drink; never would I cross the threshold of the public-house again."

My friend laughed as he came to this part of his story. "I signed the pledge, sir, but it was in a new fashion, too—perhaps never a temperance pledge was signed that way before. I was sitting there in the mist and shadow of that side of the river, and there came a flock of ducks right down within easy shot. I was thinking about the pledge, and never saw them till they were right on to me. Then I put my gun to the shoulder, and in a minute more I should have had a brace, but that very second it come into my mind that the public-house where I met my mates was called *The Wild Drake.* 'You shall go,' I cried out, half laughing as I said it—'go for a token that by God's help I have done with *The Wild Drake* for ever and ever.' Well, I knew I should make short work of the old company, and of the old ways, too, as soon as I had done with the drink. Then I thought of one thing and another. I would go with mother on Sundays, and a half a dozen things came to my mind that I would have done with. My heart began to beat with a kind of a pride. It was grand to be getting into a good man all so quickly, and so easy, too. Why, if I went on like this I should get into a saint. The cry of the ducks overhead and the whistle of the curlews were nothing to me now. Was there anything else that I could do, for I was going to make a clean sweep? It was no use playing at it. Half and half would only mean the old ways back again very soon. If I was going to turn over a new leaf, it must be all as smooth and white and clean as it could be. My resolution seemed to grow with every new surrender, and all my heart was lighter and gladder for everything that I gave up. My whole life should be changed, and this new year should have a brighter tale to tell than any I had ever lived before. Then I thought I would push off the boat and get away home, and tell the dear old mother what I meant to do.

"Ah, sir, I can never forget it. I had pushed off and turned round homeward, and just settled to the oars, feeling as if everything was right—wind and tide and all was fair. There, right in front of me, was the glistening water, stretching like a sheet of silver away towards the moon. In an instant it all flashed back upon me as plain as I ever saw anything in my life. I could see the cabin-boy with his pale

face and his hands stretched out, and I seemed to
hear his cry again—'IT WON'T SINK!' I had been
clearing the hold, pitching the cargo into the sea,
but there it was ; right away behind me, like as if it
stretched up to the very throne of God, there was
every word that I had ever spoken; everything I
had ever done, every wish I had ever felt—there it
lay, right out in the light of God. My soul sank
down in helplessness and horror. *It won't sink!*
were the words that kept ringing over and over
again in my ears.

"I just flung myself at the oars with a desperate
fierceness. It was no good my trying—not a bit. It
did not matter what I did; there seemed nothing
else for it but to give right in to everything that was
bad. Whatever I did, wherever I went, there was
all the past stretching out before God—nothing forgotten! nothing buried! It was no use playing the
fool like this any longer—clearing the hold when the
cargo wouldn't sink. Tears filled my eyes, partly
because all my hopes were gone, and partly because I
was so helpless to make things any better. I just
pulled away fierce and almost mad, wishing with
every stroke of the oars that I could get down under
the water and end it all.

"Everything seemed to mock me. The great
moon shone all so still and bright, as if it were
nothing at all that anybody should be tossed and

driven away like my soul was. The mud itself, the ugly, useless mud, shone all silvery in the light, as if somehow it was possible for everything to be better except me. So on in that stillness I went, feeling the wretchedest soul that ever lived, just as if I was dragging that dreadful past after me with every stroke of the oars. The ringing of the bells came across the water again, but there was no music in it for me. What was the good of ringing out the old year and ringing in the new, when year in and year out there was all my life lying out like that before God! I couldn't undo a thing of it, couldn't unsay a word! It seemed a mockery to ring bells in a world like this.

" But as I pulled on the fierceness died out of me, until all that I felt was a great burden of helplessness. My hold of the oars grew slacker and slacker, until I stopped pulling altogether, and just drifted with the tide. Tears filled my eyes and rolled down my cheeks. I looked right away up into the heavens— there was only a star or two shining, but somehow it made me feel that God was looking down on me, and surely, I thought, He must pity me. Could I not kneel down and tell Him all about it, and ask Him to help me ? And my mother's saying came to my mind—that prayer is stronger than the devil and sin. I pulled into a bit of 'hard' where I could land, and made my boat fast. Then I went away to a bit of rocky cliff by the riverside, underneath an old tree. I kneeled down and began to pray. I just pleaded guilty to it all. 'There it lies, Lord, floating out under Thine eye, all the past,' I cried in my distress. I told Him that I did want to start afresh, but that it was no use if I had always to go dragging the past after me like this. I did not like to ask the Lord to sink it all, but I did ask Him what he could do with it. The more I prayed the more sure I felt that He would help me. I had forgotten all about the time, and just kneeled on in prayer. How long I had been there I can't tell, perhaps for an hour or more. Then all in a moment, I don't know how, but I could sooner doubt my own life than doubt this. It was like a blaze of light on my mind—everything was as clear as day. The Lord Jesus Christ had come on purpose to deliver me from that past. It was gone—all gone. It was all cut off and sunk. I looked, and it was as if I could see across the shining water, and there was not a speck upon it, not one black sin left floating there. My sins were buried in the depths of the sea. I shouted for joy. No poor condemned prisoner ever felt so glad at his escape as I did that night. The past was *sunk*—no eye could see it; none could ever find it again; it was gone, to be remembered against me no more for ever. Turn where I would it was brightness and calm. There was no condemnation. Once again I looked up, with my eyes filled with tears, but they were tears of joy this time.

" As I pushed off and began to row homeward there came again the pealing of the bells. Ah, there was music in it now, music that my own soul answered to, for all the joy bells of my heart were ringing their very sweetest.

" So that is what came out of that summer morn‧ing's adventure. And that is how I began the New Year, thank God, and how I began a new life, too. I have very often thought of it since, and said to myself—" *It is no good clearing the hold if the cargo won't sink.*' "

Bob.

CHAPTER I.

HOW I CAME TO KNOW HIM.

I FIRST met my good friend Bob at a temperance
meeting in which he and I were to take part as

speakers. I had previously been attending another
meeting, and had to come from a distant part of the
city in a cab, winding in and out through the misty
darkness until I found myself set down on a quay,
where I could dimly make out chains and ropes and
all the signs of shipping. A friendly hand piloted
me across the gangway, and along the deck of a
vessel, until I reached a narrow, winding staircase,
down which I felt my way through the darkness.
Then, as a door was flung open, a blaze of light fell
on me suddenly, and I found myself in the midst of
the meeting. It was a large place, in which nearly
a thousand persons must have been gathered. The
sides of the long, low room were decorated with the
flags of all nations ; and this, as well as the faces and
dress of most of the audience, and the whole tone and
freedom of the meeting, suggested the heartiness of
the sailor. The songs were lustily applauded, and
the chorus was rung out with that rollicking vigour
which no one understands so well as Jack ashore.
The very speeches seemed irresistibly to catch a kind
of nautical flavour, and the illustrations came from
the sea.

This was the Bethel ship at B——, of old a sloop of
war known as the *Etna*. She had done her share of
fighting in the Chinese seas, and then had come
home to lie in easy indolence with many another
fighting companion in Plymouth Sound. But sud-

denly the career of the *Etna* was completely
changed. She was purchased of the Government
for 1500*l.*, and converted into a preaching-place for
sailors.

A wonderful power attended the earliest services
that were held on board. At almost every meeting
souls were stricken down in a bitter conviction of
sin ; and in the cockpit, where of old time the poor
fellows lay wounded and groaning, now the broken-
hearted kneeled crying to God ; and there the Good
Physician came and made them whole, and sent them
on the way rejoicing. The fame of the services went
forth, bringing many more ; and to this day there
are scores of earnest Christian people who look back
to those memorable services on board the Bethel ship
as the date of their great change. It would be hard
to find any stories more striking or more wonderful
than some of these conversions—stories of men who
had gone down to the very lowest depths of sin
plucked as brands from the burning, and becoming in
turn amongst the most zealous and successful of
Christian workers.

But suddenly all thought alike of the ship and her
captain was cut short, as amidst a boisterous applause
from the audience the chairman called upon "Mr.
E——." But the name that passed from one to another of the audience was much shorter and more
familiar. "Bob," said everybody to everybody else,

with a nod of eager expectation, and then everybody settled down into a dead silence.

There stood forward a man, not very tall, but very broad; a large round head with thick stubby hair; a face clean shaven; no neck to speak of, but the head coming at once on to a pair of huge shoulders which were fitted with arms and hands to match. Everything about the man suggested at the first sight something pugilistic. But a second glance made one doubtful—the firm and prominent brows came down over a pair of the kindliest eyes, and as he began to speak the face was lit up with a radiance such as made me feel that whatever the man was once, he lived now full in the sunshine, and kept that strong square-set face of his turned up toward it the whole day through.

Bob's voice was husky and inclined to run into the falsetto. You felt that a man of such strength must have been able some time or other to roar like a bull —probably had indeed—and spent so much of his voice in riotous living that he now had to use what was left of it very sparingly, and could only find the remnants in odd out-of-the-way corners of the vocal regions. It needed only half an eye to see that Bob, like the Bethel ship, had once been in a very different line from this in which I first came to know him.

"Friends, I believe what the chairman said is true," he began. "There is nothing in all the world so mighty as love. Why, bless you! if you can only make anybody feel that you love them, you can just do anything with them—seeming to me that that is God's way of saving the world. I know that is how He saved me—bless His name!—and I know that is how we can help to save other people too. There, I was marching along with the Salvation Army percession last Tuesday was a week since, and when we come up opposite to the bridge there was a man stood there about a 'three sheets in the wind,' as the saying is, and he tried to break the ranks, rolling up against one and another.

"Well, I steps up to him so gentle as I could. 'Friend,' I says, 'you must not go a-doing that, you know. Please don't.'

"Then he turns round and wants to know who I was, and begins to swear and square up to me, and all of a sudden he turns round and was just a-going to lurch in upon the percession again.

"Well, friends, I put up my hand just so," and Bob held up a hand that might have belonged to Samson or even to Goliath of Gath. "I just puts up my hand, and of course down he goes in a minute." It certainly was a result of which no one who saw the hand could have the slightest doubt. "Well, so soon as ever he was down, I picks him up again and I puts my arm round his neck: 'Eh, but I do love you,' I says."

We had laughed at Bob's way of showing his love, but as he spoke the tears glistened in his eyes, and amidst our laughter we found our eyes, too, were brimming, as with an indescribable tenderness and simplicity he went on, "'You know, I would die to do you good,' I says, 'and the Lord Jesus Christ loves you a thousand times better than I do.' Well, what does he do but takes hold of my hand, and he looks up in my face, and says he, 'Will you let a chap like me go along with you?'

"'We just will that,' I says, 'and welcome.' So I put my arm in his to steady him a bit, and away we went to the Salvation Circus. Well, that night he began to seek the Lord. Every night of the week he come-up praying for himself and us praying with him, till last Sunday night he jumps up shouting, Hallelujah! Then presently he stops—stops quite still for ever so long, like as if he couldn't speak. And then, as the tears come streaming down his cheeks, says he, in a kind of whisper, 'Friends, will you please for to praise the Lord for saving a man like me?' and he held up his hand. 'I am 'shamed for to own it, but that is the hand of the worst wife-beater in the city, and yet the Lord have saved *me.*'

"Ah, friends, 'tis true, there is nothing in the world like love. Love is almighty, like God Himself."

But this was the introduction only. Bob's speech itself was the story of his own life, as thrilling a narrative as I ever heard. Altogether I found myself quite taken with this specimen of muscular Christianity, and his touching simplicity and tenderness. Then and there I made up my mind to hear it all over again if I could only get the chance. So it came about that not very long afterwards Bob sat at my fireside, and went over it all once more in a quiet and leisurely way.

CHAPTER II.

BOB'S STORY.

I was born and reared in St. Philip's—such rearing as it was; for you see I was left to do the most part of that for myself. Neither father nor mother never took much account of us children—except when we vexed them by coming in their way, and then they took more account of us than we cared for, by a good deal. Father used to drink, and when he was drunk we was very glad to get out of the way; and when he wasn't, you might be sure that there wasn't much that was worth going home for.

One of the earliest things that I can remember is seeing the boys and girls going into the Sunday-school, and hearing them sing. They all looked so nice and clean, and it sounded so pretty, that I thought I should like to go too, and I wondered if they would give me some decent clothes like the rest had. So one Sunday afternoon I crept to the door and looked in. Somebody came up and asked me what I wanted. I told him that I did long to come to school and learn to sing with the rest. But he told me to run away home and get a clean shirt and another jacket, and then he shut the door. Bless you, why I hadn't got another in the world. I did think it was a bit hard.

" How old were you ? " I asked.

Not more than seven. It seemed to me then like as if there was nothing for it but just to get away with the wild lads that was up to all kinds of mischief upon the Lord's day, wandering about the streets.

" The devil's Sunday-school," I put in.

You may well call it that, Bob went on ; he will take all comers. Well, you see it was all gambling, and swearing and like that till I come to be thirteen or fourteen years old. A big boy I was, too, and very strong ; and a set of men got hold of me, and began to back me to fight. I was always at it. But it was a miserable life, always knocking somebody about, and then all the money spent in drink. I got so sick of it that I ran away from them and went to sea aboard a ship that traded to South Africa. But

the captain of her, he come somehow to know about
my fighting, and nothing would do but that he must
put me in training, and backed me against a full-
grown man of his crew, and the first time we landed
they made the ring and I had to fight it out.

Well, I come home again and then I was out of a
berth. It did look like as if there was nothing else
for it, and very soon I was back among the old set
again, drinking and fighting. I was seventeen year
old when I gave myself right up to it, and went
about the country with a set of boxing men. The
Herefordshire Chicken they called him, he took a
fancy to me. I used to go about with him to the
different fairs, and put on the gloves against all
comers.

Well, it went on like that till I was nineteen
years old, and then I married. Ah, my wife is a
downright good woman, sir, as ever lived. I should
like for you to see her. There isn't a woman in the
world that have gone through what she have gone
through, and stuck to anybody like she have stuck
to me. She wasn't exactly what you call converted
in those days, but she had been brought up by good
parents, and wanted always to live a good life. I
went along pretty steady with her for some months
after I was married ; but then, bit by bit, I got back
with the old set again, until I was just so bad as
ever. Then nothing would do but I must go in for

E

a regular fight, twenty-five pounds a side, along with a man they called " B—— E——."

Ah, I always think that it was all because the dear wife kept praying for me that it come about like it did. The day come that I was to send in the challenge. I was sitting in the public-house —"The Dove," it was called, of all the pretty names in the world. I had been drinking all the morning, but I wasn't so far gone but what I could manage to see that the challenge was put all straight enough.

Well, while I was sitting there amongst them, cursing and swearing and drinking, and thinking about nothing but the fight, the public-house door was opened, and in come my sister's little girl. She pushes her way in amongst them all, looking about for me. " Please is uncle here ? " she says.

I didn't want to be disturbed then, for all I loved the little 'un—a pretty little thing she was, too, as ever anybody set eyes on—so I says, " Run away home," I says, " there's a dear."

Some of the others spoke out sharp to her and began to swear at her, but I wouldn't have nothing of that.

Then the little 'un she comes right up to me and puts her little hand upon my arm, and could hardly speak for crying.

"Run home," I says again, putting her back so

gentle as I could. "Run home to your mother; uncle is busy now."

But the little 'un she presses herself up against my side and hides her face on my arm and bursts out crying, "Please, uncle, mother is dying, and she wants to see you directly."

"All right, my dear," I says, "tell mother I'll come directly." And I stroked her hair and tried to cheer her up.

But there stood the little 'un, sobbing, at my side. "Please, uncle, mother said you must come now, or she would never see you again," and the hot tears come dropping down upon my hand.

Of course I hadn't got the heart to be rough with the little 'un, and it was no good trying to coax her away, and when some of them was going to push her out, I put my arm round her and jumped up. "All right, lads," I said; "I shall be back in a minute. Don't go away."

When I got to the house there was my poor sister lying very ill; it was plain enough that she was dying. She couldn't speak much above a whisper; but it seemed like as if every word went sinking down into my heart and stayed there. I went over by her side and sat down. She took my hand in both of hers, so hot and white and wasted they were, poor dear!

"Bob," she says, "I shan't be here very long, and you was always very good to me. There's the two dear children; it is the only thing that frets me. You see Jim" (that was her husband, you know), "Jim is getting worse and worse with the drink. You will see to them, won't you, Bob?"

Poor dear! of course I promised her that I would. Then I began to think about the men that were waiting for me over to the public-house, and for all I was very sorry to leave her, I knew that it wouldn't do to keep them any longer than I could help. But she wouldn't let go of my hand—only lay there looking at me without a word for ever so long. Then all of a sudden she says quite solemn—

"Bob, will you try for to meet me in heaven? I know that I'm going there."

"I'm sure you are, my dear," I says; and I did wish that I was only as right for it as she was.

Then she went back in a kind of faint, and I thought she was gone. Presently she opens her eyes and looks at me again. "You will promise me, won't you, Bob?"

So I stooped down and kissed her, and said I would, never thinking about what I said, except to please her.

Well, as soon as I could I got up and went away back to the *Dove* again, and thought I would finish the challenge. I had my hand on the door and my foot on the threshold, when it was like as if a voice spoke to me—

" *This isn't the way to heaven—in here.*"

I stopped and turned all of a cold sweat, for I saw then what I had done.

"Meet her in heaven!" I said. "You are a ruined man, Bob, body and soul—that's plain." But there, my word was gone, and I must stick to that, of course.

Well, there was nothing else for it. I could never set foot in the place again. So I just left them to finish the challenge the best way they could without me, and I come away down the street to my house, feeling the lonesomest, miserablest man that ever lived. For days after that I could just do nothing at all. Poor dear sister was dead and gone, and I had promised to meet her in heaven. How ever was a man like me to get there? I felt that I was too bad to pray, much more to hope, and I didn't know however I could set to work to make myself any better. I was getting miserabler every day, and my life seemed to get blacker every time I looked back upon it. There was nothing that I had ever said or done, but it seemed to come back and mock me, and seemed to say, " *You* talk about trying to get to heaven—a man like you ! "

Then the old enemy would keep a-flinging it in my teeth about what a fool I was to give up such chances as I had, and all for nothing but to go about moping and groaning day and night. What had I got to do with going to heaven?—that was for sick folks and dying, like poor dear sister was. And there, if I was made stronger, and bigger, and quicker-hitting than other folks, of course it was meant to fight with—like other men was born parsons and doctors. As for being religious I might as well give that up first as last, for the old set would be coming round me again after a bit, and I should be so bad as ever. And, of course, the good folks knew all about me right enough, and they would never have anything to do along with a chap like me.

So day and night I went wondering if there was anybody in the world who could help a poor soul to get to heaven. Bless the Lord I soon found that there was. One evening I was going down the street, when a man I knew came up to me and said, " Bob, the best thing you can do is to come along with me to the cottage prayer-meeting." It was the first time that anybody had ever spoke to me about anything religious, and I thought that the Lord must have sent him a-purpose, or he never would have done it then. Of course, I was glad enough to go —the prayer-meeting was down in Sloper's lane, in a cottage there. The Methodists it was that used to hold it—in those days they used to have them all over the city. Well, so soon as I got inside the door, the leader of the meeting had given out the hymn, and they were just going to sing it, when he turns round and looks at me. "Friends," says he, turning over the pages of the hymn-book, "we must choose another."

Then he gives out the hymn—

> " God moves in a mysterious way
> His wonders to perform ;
> He plants His footsteps in the sea,
> And rides upon the storm."

I don't know what it was—can't account for it in any way at all—but I just heard the verse, and then all of a sudden I was knocked down to the floor— blind, and like anybody dead. They took me up, thinking at first that I was dead, and then carried me out in the air, and fetched water, and all that, and after an hour or so I come round again. But from that moment everything was worse than ever. Turn where I would my sins stared me in the face and filled me with terror. I was almost afraid to put my foot to the ground for fear it should let me through into hell—and then I should set to almost wishing that I could die and get away from my misery.

Well, so it went on until the Thursday evening. By that time a good many of them had come to know that I was seeking the Lord, and two or three come round to take me up to a house where a Methodist class-meeting was held. And there, that night— ah ! I shall never forget the very spot—whilst they were praying and talking with me, and telling me about the love of God and the Cross of Christ, the blessed Spirit just gave me to see it all—how that God loved *me*, and the blessed Jesus had died for my sins. My soul was full of peace and light, the storm and the tempest was over, and there was nothing but the still small voice a-telling me of God's love. I was another man. No two men in this world ever felt so different or looked so different as I did that night when I went in and when I came out. It was a new world, and I was a new man in it. Everything was different. Heaven—an hour before it was farther off than the sun, and now it was a sort of just in next door, and I might step in through the gate at any moment. I went home so soon as I could to the dear wife to tell her all about it, and for the first time in our lives we knelt down together before the Lord, and gave thanks to Him. It was June, that was the month, in the year 1849 ; I shall never forget that day. And for many a day afterwards there was not a happier man in God's world than I was.

So comes the pleasant scene of the happy home, surely of all scenes the very pleasantest. There was the love and trust of husband and wife hallowed as they kneeled together in prayer with the little ones.

For the children themselves there came a hundred
new delights. There were little bits of comfort and
even luxury that the wages purchased now. There
was the new and blessed gladness of the Sunday as
they went together to worship, joining in hymns that
seemed to keep the heart in tune for a week, bending
together in prayer and over the Word, and knit
together in a new and hallowed union by the Father's
love to them, and by the hope of heaven. Sweetness
and gentleness made all the round of life like another
world ; the children came and went light-hearted, love
always waited at home for them now, and as for the
good wife, cared for with such a tenderness, life
seemed almost too full of joy for her. And over all
there rested the favour of God, in the house, and
family, and work, warming and gladdening it like a
perpetual summer.

"I was just as happy as the day was long," Bob
went on. "And more than that, too, for so soon as
the day was done we was always trying to get a bit
of good, or to do a bit, somewhere. There was my
old mates, I did long to see them brought to the
Lord. Very often they would come round me and
try to worry me ; but I never felt any inclination for
to knock them down, nor nothing of that : my heart
was full of love to them, every one. I did sometimes tell them that they might thank the Lord that
it was with me as it was, or they would know the

difference pretty quick. But it was never no more than that. There, I couldn't help loving everybody —friends and enemies, it was all alike."

CHAPTER III.

"THERE'S NO HARM IN IT."

WELL, I went on like that for four years. Ah! I little thought that ever the bad old times would come again, and specially that they would come back like they did, too. The people that I joined along with was the nicest and brotherliest that ever could be— they were always trying to do everybody a good turn and to lend a helping hand. And such happy times as we used to have, too, singing and praying in each other's houses, and asking the neighbours to come in and join us. Often and often God's power would come down upon and fill the place, and poor souls would be finding peace and joy in believing.

It come to Whit Tuesday, and in those days they used to have a great meeting over to K——, a "love-feast" they called it. People would go miles to it, and the place would be crowded. The leader of our class, that is the man who looked after us a bit, was going over, and we all agreed to walk over with him, and we were to call for him directly after dinner. Well, we got to the house and knocked at the door. " Come in," says he, " I shall have done in a minute."

So soon as ever I got in and sat down, there I saw him take up a glass of liquor and drain it off. I was quite frightened, and almost jumped off my chair. Then I looked round to the others to see if they were so frightened as I was, but they didn't seem to take any notice of it. He was a good man, I was sure of that—so good a man as ever stepped. But I never knew before that good people ever touched that kind of stuff. You see I had always thought of it as the source of almost all the devilry and mischief and wretchedness that there was in the world. "It can't be so dreadfully bad then after all," I says to myself, when I had got a bit over my fright, " else he wouldn't be touching it, of course."

As we went along together I could think of nothing else. At last I began to talk about it. " Do you think a glass of that liquor would do me any harm ?" I says.

" Well, that depends," says he. " There's some folks that can take it, and there's some that can't. If you can take it there's no harm in it, not a bit."

" Oh, I can take it right enough," I says.

Well, we went to the meeting, but somehow the words kept coming to me all the time, " *There's no harm in it, not a bit.*" One and another told what dreadful drunkards they had been, and how that the grace of God had saved them. But then I thought that was all because they couldn't take it.

The next day I went to work, but somehow there wasn't so much light and singing in my soul as usual. "You want a glass of liquor," says the enemy; "there's no harm in it, not a bit."

Well, I tried to argue it over with him, but the old tempter shut me up in a minute. "Don't you set up to know better than Mr. B——. He is a good man, he is a better man than you will ever be, and he says *there is no harm in it, not a bit.*"

Every time I passed a public-house door the devil would keep pulling and tugging at me. "Why shouldn't you have a glass? there is no harm in it.' For a week I did not give in. Then I suddenly came upon an old friend that I had not seen for a long time.

"Come in and have a glass of beer, Bob," says he.

It was just all I was wanting—that friendly word settled it.

"Well," I says, "I don't mind if I do. They tell me there is no harm in it."

"Harm! I should think not," laughed the man— a goodish sort of man he was, too.

So I found myself inside the public-house again. I didn't feel at all comfortable, the old ways seemed to be a good deal nearer to anybody inside than they were outside. But the words came back again—it was the last time I needed them—*there is no harm in it, not a bit.*

That was the beginning of it. All my desire after good things just went right away there and then. That was the beginning of it, but nobody will never know what the end of it was except God Himself. No harm in it! The devil himself could not have wished for more.

In a month from that time I was back again, worse than ever I had been. With that first glass the longing for it came upon me. And it got worse and worse, until day and night I began to be craving for the drink. All the happy ways went long before the month was done, all the sunshine, and all the love, and everything like that, and what was best and dearest to me in all the world came in now for the biggest share of abuse and misery. I was mad with myself for being such a fool, and instead of stopping me, that only drove me oftener to the drink. It was like as if now I had given in to it, the only way to be easy in it was to be always at it. Bit by bit the little things about the house went for drink, till in a drunken fit all that was left was smashed. The pretty little place that used to look so nice, and that the dear wife took such a pride in, was all torn to rack and ruin. There was not so much as a chair to sit down on, or a cup to drink out of.

Poor Bob stopped and turned his eye away from me, he looked out of the window and shook his head sadly. " *No harm in it!* " he sighed to himself. It was evident that the scenes of those sad times were crowding back upon him. After a few minutes he turned to me again.

" So it went on worse and worse till there was no worse to be got to. Week in and week out it was all blows and cursing. Look here, sir," and as he spoke he leaned forward and put his finger on the white scars that showed out from between the thick stubby hair, " that is where I have had my head split open in drunken brawls many a time."

Again he was quiet. I began to think that the dreadful monotony of bad years had left no further incident to be told. Presently he turned to me again, and went on in a sadder tone—

And there was the poor dear children! Ah, many a time they would come to dinner—and there was nothing but a bit of dry bread, and sometimes not even that—ragged and starved, and often obliged to run away anywhere so soon as they heard me coming, poor little dears. And again Bob sighed to himself, " *No harm in it!* "

Then came another pause, longer than any. Again Bob looked out of the window with a vacant look. He kept his eyes fixed on the distance as he began again speaking in almost a whisper. " The dear wife stuck to me through it all. It seemed like as if she couldn't leave me, no matter how bad I was; and, if she had, I should have been lost, lost for ever and ever." The eyes filled with tears as Bob went on. "Stuck to me through it all; would come trying to get me out of the public-house. And "—(the tears came trickling down his cheeks, and his voice sank to a whisper)—"I beat her, poor dear, beat her sir."

The strong arm leaned on the table, and the huge hand hung over the edge of it. I shuddered to think of that fist lifted savagely at any woman. The voice sank to a husky whisper, and the tears came more thickly on his cheeks.

"I beat her, sir. I should never know it till next morning, and mad enough I should be with myself, too, when I saw how I had knocked her about. One time she was so bad that they could give her nothing but spoon-meat for eleven days. And for all that she wouldn't leave me." Bob sighed again more deeply than ever, and as he wiped his eyes, he muttered to himself, "*No harm in it!*"

Then Bob turned to me again. "It wasn't once, nor twice, but it went on like that for years. And then when I was a poor cast-away, with nothing left —no character, no money, no hope, nothing—and was standing on the very brink of hell, then it was that God's mercy met me again. It is all so wonderful as ever, whenever I think about it, for all I have looked back upon it so many times.

I had got down so low and so mad, that one night I made up my mind to end it all. The little place was stript; the poor dear wife was nearly heart-broken; the children would be better without any father than one like they had; there was no chance of my ever mending, so I might as well finish it first as last. It was a beautiful night—the moon was full, and the light came right into the room where we was sleeping, so that it was all so clear as day. I gets up, and takes my razor and sharpens it up so well as I could. Then I came over to the bed. There was she lying asleep. And I stood there thinking how nice she looked, and what a brute I had been to her; and how much better it would be for her and me too, if I was to end it all.

Well, while I was standing there like that, the dear wife just opens her eyes and looks up all so kind and gentle, like as if I had never lifted my hand on her in my life.

" Why, Bob, dear," she says, " whatever are you going to do ? "

It just broke my heart. I fell down to the ground, and could do nothing but cry almost all the rest of the night. So soon as it was day I got up and slipped away, and made up my mind to drown my griefs in the drink. It was Sunday morning. I had wandered about a bit, until it came eleven o'clock or so, and I was going up over the hill. The streets were very quiet, and there was nobody about just then, and as I come to the top of the hill I heard a voice speak to me so plain as ever I heard anything in my life—" Take and go back to chapel, Bob."

" No," I said, " they will all laugh at me if I do." And I turned round to see who it was, but there was nobody there. And whilst I was wondering whatever it could mean, the voice spoke to me again— " Take and go down to Major T——'s chapel; they don't know you down there."

What it was I am sure I can't tell, only I felt quite sure that it was one more chance of salvation for me. It seemed too much to think about, much more to hope for. However, straight away I went to the major's chapel. I crept inside the door, hoping that nobody would see me, when the old major stopped and looked all about the place.

" I think there is a poor backslider here this morning," he said, and it was like as if he set his eye upon me. " I want to tell him that God is going to restore his soul."

Of course I thought he must know me, and I tried to get up and go out, but it seemed like as if I couldn't. My heart was broken as the thought of my sin came crushing in upon me, and I could only put my face down in my hands and cry.

F

Well, so soon as the service was done I got up and
started for home. When I come near to the door of
our house I heard the little boy call out, " Mother,
he's coming."

Poor dear wife. I heard her say, "Is he
drunk ? "

" No, mother," says the little fellow ; " he do look
like as if he been crying," and then he was off.

Ah! it was crying and crying and keeping on crying for many a day after that. I could do nothing
else, how could I ? I felt myself such a brute beast
that I could not sit down to meat with my wife and
children for weeks after that. I was ashamed to let
them see me. I used to take my bit of victuals and
go away by myself, away out in the yard, or upstairs
—anywhere out of sight. I didn't feel that I could
ask God to forgive me. I didn't want Him to. I
wanted Him to keep me smarting and weeping for it.
But He did forgive me, bless His name! almost
before I asked Him to, and a very long time before I
could forgive myself. And as for the poor dear wife,
she made it harder than ever, for it was nothing but
goodness and love from her.

Well, then I found my way back to the class. It
was just like the prodigal coming home. The dear
old leader, he flung his arms about my neck and
kissed me, and they all praised the Lord for me.
They told me that never a day had passed since I had

gone away from them, but they had prayed the Lord to bring me back again.

"Bless the Lord! I knew He would," cried the dear old leader, and he could do nothing but wipe his eyes and praise the Lord.

"A good man he was, I am sure of that," said Bob as he rose to go, "and I never blamed him for what he did. He meant well enough."

"Well," said I, "meaning right won't go far unless it is backed up by doing right. I DON'T THINK IT IS RIGHT FOR GOOD FOLKS TO GO PLAYING WITH LUCIFER MATCHES WHEN THERE ARE SO MANY POWDER MAGAZINES ABOUT."

"Strike While the Iron's Hot."

My old friend Nath, the village blacksmith, was a man worth knowing. Whether you wanted a well-made horse-shoe, or a bit of shrewd and pleasant common-sense, you would have to go a long way before you could find yourself better suited with either than at his smithy. Sturdy and strong and true, he had a way of holding himself upright in God's world, partly from a natural independence, but mostly because he knew whose world it is, being quite sure that it is well put together, and that Love and Wisdom are always trying to lead men on to some goodness and worth.

No man knew better than he that life has in it fierce fires, and sharp blows, and stern things that are mysterious, perhaps, and hard to bear; but out of his own forge there shot many a side-light that lit up darker matters than the smithy itself; and out of the iron, as it rang on his anvil, came lessons that were more than the music it made.

" Things are not put together haphazard and any-how, lads," said old Nath, as he worked away; " this bit of iron thought it was meant to be let alone nice and comfortable, and it can't think why it should be hit about and hammered at like this"; and as he spoke he gripped the iron with the big pincers and thrust it into the sleepy fire, and then, laying hold of the handle of the bellows, he made the dull red coals wake up with a roar as the white flames leapt up the chimney and the sparks flew in showers over the smithy roof and trailed away in the black December night. But the iron made a mistake if it thought that there was nothing else that had to do with it but a great pair of sinewy arms and the fierce blast of the bellows and the roaring fire. Those same white flames lit up as kindly a face as ever was stained with smoke and dust—a cheery face from which no little child would ever shrink, and lads and maidens coming home from school on these winter evenings were sure of a welcome as they stood to warm their blue hands about old Nath's fire. The sight of old Nath himself was almost enough to send the glass up to a comfortable degree whichever way the wind blew, as those kind eyes looked at you from behind the big-rimmed spectacles. His mouth had curled and twisted itself into wrinkles and dimples that were all so many traps for smiles and good humour; and away behind that brawny chest he carried a heart so big that it held a bit of true love for everybody living.

But alas! how could the iron believe all this?— played on by those fierce fires, and gripped by those great pincers, and now hurried away to the anvil; and then the big arms smite at it mightily, making the sparks fly about the place; and then off to the dark corner where the trough stood, and dipped into the icy water, making the tormented thing hiss and sputter until old Nath was almost hidden in the steam. Then, as the iron is wondering whatever it can have done to be dealt with like this, and whether it ever is going to be let alone again, old Nath turns round and hangs the finished horse-shoe up beside many others, and rests his pincers on the anvil.

"Poor stuff iron would be if it had never a fire to soften it, lads, or a hammer to hit it, or an anvil to shape it on," says old Nath, cheerily. "I hear it sputtering and hissing in the water as if it didn't like it; but, bless you, the horse-shoe will sing about it some day when it goes ringing merrily on the high road. 'Click, clack,' it will sing, 'click, clack. Ride on, master; you won't wear me out in a hurry; for didn't old Nath smite me on his anvil, and dip me in that bath of his, and he made me hardened and toughened and strong?'" Then old Nath spoke more gravely—"Aye, lads, and if folks would only believe it, there's a good many besides horse-shoes that will come to sing some day about fire and hammer and things they don't like, if they will only let the Master have His own way with them, and let Him work out what He wants. Smiths are plentier than people think in God's world, and most of us need as much hitting as the iron does before we are any good." Nath shrugged his shoulder as he spoke, as if he had not far to go for an illustration. "Rheumatics and aches of all sorts, and worries and losses and sorrows, are all helping to shape us, if we will only hold ourselves right to them, and not go flying off like a clinker instead of a bit of real stuff."

.   .   .   .   .   .

It was the last day of the year, a time when grave thoughts come naturally to people who are much less

used to think than was old Nath. As the evening
closed in, a group of young men belonging to the
village were gathered in the smithy. The hum of
voices, the ring of the anvil, the roar of the bellows,
filled the place. Old Nath had leaned for some
minutes over the fire, quietly meditating. Now he
drew out of the flames a piece of iron, white and
glowing, and held it up on high.

"There, lads," he cried, " look at that."

The noise of the voices was hushed instantly, and
every face was turned to the glowing metal. Its
white light fell on the ring of faces that gathered
behind the apprentice.

"You can make anything of that now," old Nath
went on. " You can beat it and bend it and shape it
to bolt or bar, nut or screw ; a score of uses are in it.
But let it alone, and in a little time it will be hard
and past working. Ah, my lads, that's like the New
Year that lies before us all. To-night it will be your
own to make of it what you will, by God's help ; but
you may let it alone, and it will be a thing turned to
no account—a stone instead of iron. Will you let
me preach you a sermon, and take this bit of iron for
a text ? I won't trouble you with any firstlies and
secondlies, and I promise you that it shan't be very
long, and I hope it won't be very dull." Then old
Nath added devoutly, " And may God bless the word
to our hearts."

" 'Tis five-and-thirty years ago to-night, the last night of the year. When you have heard my story you won't wonder that I can think of nothing else. I had been wed a year; aye, and when I married her, there wasn't a bonnier lass in the land, not to my thinking, anyhow. As tall and as straight as a larch, and with such roses in her cheeks, and such sunshine in her eyes, and a voice that sang so sweet that I used to go to church on purpose to hear her." Old Nath sighed. " It was the only thing that could ever take me in those times; and sit where I would, I could always hear it, so sweet and clear; it did me more good than sermon or service, for I didn't think about listening to them then.

" Only twelve months after, and the last day of the year had come again—ah, the roses were faded, the light had died, the music was gone. There she sat in the little cottage with the baby at her breast —a ghost of a baby it was, and she but a shadow of what she used to be.

" Well, that night I had done my supper, and rose up to get ready for the night's work. I was going towards the door, ragged and half drunk, for I had begun pretty early in the afternoon 'to see the old year out,' as they called it. Then the lass gets up and hurries round in front of me, and she spoke like as if it were her old self come back, all so light-hearted and cheerful.

"'Nath,' she says, 'wilt kiss the little one before you go, and say good-night to him?'

"I kissed him, but roughly, and he cried, and she took him back to her breast. She was standing in front of me, and she put her hand on my shoulder and took hold of my coat.

"'Wilt kiss me too, Nath?' she said; and her voice trembled a little.

"I wondered rather what she meant, but was in a hurry to go, so I kissed her. As I stooped she put her hand about my neck, and the tears filled her eyes. She put her face against me, and couldn't speak for a little bit. Presently, without looking up, but putting her arm tighter about me, she whispered, 'I wish you wouldn't go to-night—for his sake, and—and for mine.'

"I felt a bit soft-like, she hanging there about me and crying so, and the tears were coming more quickly. Then she looked up into my face. '*Don't, don't* go to-night,' she sobbed: 'if you do, I shall never see you again. I've dreamt about it night after night."

"'Well,' I said, gently putting off her arm, " you see I must go and tell the others, or they will be waiting for me."

"She saw I meant to go, and her face grew paler than ever. 'Say good-bye to him again,' she said, holding up the baby. Then she turned away and sat down by the fire.

"It did come to me for a minute to stay at home

with her and the little one, for it went to my heart to
see her all so pale and sad. But then I thought of
the others, and how they would be waiting for me at
the public-house, and how we reckoned on a grand
bit of luck, for there was a servants' ball up at the
Court, and we knew that the keepers would be there, all
but a raw hand or so. 'No,' I said to myself, 'it is no
good ; whatever comes of it, I must go to-night.' So
I hurried out, shut the door very quietly, and went off.

" Ah, my lads, whatever better feelings came to me
inside my own door, I left them all outside the door
of the public house. The laugh and the song and
the beer soon made me forget all about the lass and
the little one at her breast. But still it was needful
to keep our heads a bit clear for the night's work,
and so to get out of the way of the drink I left them.
Our plans were all laid. We were to meet at twelve
o'clock at four cross roads, by a gate at the end of
the squire's wood. In a general way I should have
gone home to get a bit of sleep, and let the wife waken
me up, for I am a bad hand at that, and always was,
leastways in the dead of night ; but I had no heart
to go home now, so I strolled away to the meeting-
place more than hour before the time.

" To hide myself, and because I thought it would
be more comfortable, I got in over the gate and lay
in the hedge, not so far in but that I could hear the
voices of the others when they should come, but far

enough in to be well out of sight. I leaned back
against the hedge, and got away in amongst the
branches. It was a beautiful night, for the moon
was full; and though there was no wind about, yet
the long thin clouds went flying over the moon and
along the sky. All was still as still could be. Now
and then there came the cry of the owls in the wood,
or the rustle of some creature in the hedge, but it
only made the stillness greater. Then up from the
old church clock there came the strokes of the hour.
I counted one by one : it was eleven.

" 'So another year is almost gone," I said to myself. 'Another year ;' and I sighed as I said it. I
had always meant when I got married to settle down
steady and quiet, just looking in at the public-house
for a pint of beer now and then when the day's work
was done, and then home to my wife. I meant it
honestly and earnestly enough, and liked to think
what a pleasant place I was going to make for her,
and how happy we should be. I had promised it
all to the lass before we were wed. And when the
neighbours told her that she would only throw herself
away on a wild good-for-nothing, she held up her head
quite proud-like, and said that her Nath was going
to be quite different, and they would see, that they
would. Bless her, she believed it, and so did I, too.

" But there, lads, I didn't strike while the good
purpose was hot, and bit by bit it cooled, and I was

just as bad as ever. The pint led to the public-house, and the public-house led to the company, and the company led to the poaching. It was the old story over again from beginning to end ; and yet not the old story, but worse. The earnings, that had scarcely been enough for one when drink made a big hole in them, were a good deal less for two. The little place had already begun to lose some of the things that the lass had prided herself upon ; the garden that I had done up for her coming was all wilderness and weeds ; and though I, like the garden, had got smartened up a bit for the wedding, here I was, just as dirty and ragged, though the lass slaved and toiled to keep things nice and tidy. *And now was the new year going to be just the same ?*

"There in the loneliness and stillness I seemed to see again the sad, pale face and the ghost of the baby ; and when once I saw it, it just looked at me out of everything. It was in the moon and the white-edged clouds, and then it was in the very shadows that flew over me like ghosts. I seemed to feel her hand on my shoulder, and her voice at my ear ; and then I should see her far up in the clouds, as if she were gone, vanishing ever so far away in the mists. ' *Don't, don't* go to-night.' I could hear the words as plain as if she spoke again in front of me.

"And then I thought of her dream ; what did it mean ? Grim things and dreadful would sometimes happen in poaching—that I knew well enough. And then I laughed at my folly. No, some day I might see a way out of it, ' but not now,' I said to myself; ' not now.' And so in the silence and waiting, having nothing else to do, I fell asleep. Tired as I was, I slept soundly enough, and knew nothing more until I woke up, cold, and wondering what had become of the others.

" Then the old church clock struck one. So then the Old Year had gone, and the New Year was come, and the men that I had waited for had come and gone, too. I got up and hurried to the gate and listened. There was not a sound. I gave the signal which each understood, but there was no answer. Whilst I slept they must have passed by, not seeing me anywhere, and now there was no chance of my finding them. At first I was vexed enough to have missed them like this. And then there came again that pale-faced lass, and the poor little one at her breast. ' Come,' I said to myself, ' I shall be able to begin the New Year well, then, after all.'

" I turned in over the fields, and hurried across to the little cottage. As I came near, I saw, late as it was, a light shining in the window. I lifted the latch very quietly, for I dreaded to meet the lass, with her face paler and sadder for this long watching. As I came in I saw her kneeling at a chair fast asleep, with the bible open before her. A

tear was on her cheek; it glistened in the candle
light; and there was the trace of tears on the page.
There was not a sound except the quick and heavy
breathing of the baby in its cradle. The lass looked
so white, and with her hands hanging down all helpless over the chair, it was like one dead. I crept
behind her, and looked over her shoulder at the open
page. My eye fell upon the words—*" They cry unto
the Lord in their trouble, and He bringeth them out
of their distresses."*

" I cannot tell you, lads, how it came upon me,
and smote my heart. Now I saw what it meant to
her, these nights when I was away, never thinking
but what she was fast asleep in her bed. And here
she stayed up like this, praying for me, and with
tears, too! It broke my heart. I knew now what
had made her all so pale and sad, and I thinking all
the time that it was all along of the baby and her
fretting because he was so weak and ill. It was my
doing, all of it *mine*, and yet I loved the lass better
than my life.

" I kneeled down by her side. I didn't know how
to pray exactly; but I knew it would do me good to
get down beside her, and there at the open Book. I
could not say anything, only bowed my head and let
my tears of grief and shame flow down before God,
and longed with all my heart that He would make me
a better man.

"I had not kneeled long when the lass woke up with a shriek. She sprang on her feet, and threw up her clasped hands. Her eyes were wild and frightened. Then suddenly she turned round and caught sight of me kneeling there. She snatched at the candle, and looking at me as frightened as ever, put out her hand and felt me. 'Thank God,' she sobbed; 'it was a dream.'

"'What was it, lass?' I said getting up and letting her lean against me.

"She put up her hand again as if to make sure that it was me. 'I have dreamt it night after night,' she said. 'I saw a man lying under the trees, and amongst the ferns and grass, stretched cold and dead with a mark in his forehead like a picture of murdered Abel that they have got in a Bible in my father's house; but I could never see the rest of the face. Every night I have got nearer and nearer. I seemed to know who it was all the time:' and she put her hand about me more tightly; 'but to night I came right in, and stood over it, and the moon came out from a cloud and fell right on it, *and it was you, Nath,*" she said, with a shiver, and pressing against me; 'and the fright woke me up. Thank God you are here.'

"We stood quite still for some minutes. I could only think what her praying for me might have done. At any rate, it had brought me home to

begin the year aright. My voice was choked as I
spoke at last, and I could scarcely get the words
out. 'Lass,' I whispered, 'will you pray for me?
God will hear *you*. He has already.' She looked
up at me again as if it was still a dream; and
then we knelt together. And there we began that
New Year, kneeling there at the opened Bible.

" Ah, lads, before that New Year was two hours
old, I promised the lass, by God's help, to have done
with the drink altogether. It should not be a pint
nor a drop. And I put it down in writing, and the
lass signed her name to it as witness. And I
kissed her that time without her asking for it. And
though the roses hadn't had time to grow, the old
glad light came back in the eyes again. And thank
God the light has been there ever since.

" ' Ah, Nath,' said she, ' I can wish us all a Happy
New Year now.'

" My heart was too full for any words. I could
only nod my head, and mean that by God's grace it
should be that.

" And now, lads, I wish that could be the end of
my story, but it wasn't '—old Nath shook his head
sadly—' it wasn't. That night whilst I lay asleep
there came a loud knocking at the door; it was about
five o'clock in the morning, and quite dark of course.
I got up and opened the window. ' Who's there?'
I asked.

" It was the squire who spoke, but I heard the whisper of other voices near him. I could see nothing, for the moon had set, and it was raining very heavily.

" Is that you, Thompson ? " said his honour.

" ' Yes, your honour," I said, guessing at once it had something to do with the night's poaching, and thinking dreadful things.

" ' Come, you must let us in," said the gruff voice of the policeman.

" Hurrying on a few things as quickly as I could, I went down and opened the door. I had lit the candle and set it on the table. There upon the chair lay the opened Bible and the piece of paper on which I had signed the pledge.

" ' This looks very suspicious, your honour," said the policeman ; " everybody knows that Nath Thompson is no saint."

" The squire picked up the piece of paper. " May I read this ? " he asked.

" ' Well, yes, your honour," I said ; " but it wasn't meant for anybody to look at but the lass and me."

" In those times the pledge was rather a new thing. The squire read it through twice, and looked at me in wonder. He couldn't tell what to make of it. Meanwhile the policeman had taken up the boots, and seeing that there was neither rain nor mud about them, shook his head doubtfully. He felt the coat that I had thrown over me. They themselves were

dripping with the rain, but all I had on was perfectly
dry. Then the squire spoke very gravely, looking at
me the whole time, but not unkindly. 'Thompson,
perhaps you know already, perhaps you don't—and I
really don't think you know anything about it—that
there has been an attack made upon one of my keepers
to-night; we fear it will prove to be a case of
murder. One of the poachers is in custody, the
other or others have escaped. Our suspicions turned
to you."

" ' I know nothing about it, your honour," I gasped
out, horrified as my wife's dream rose before me, and
at what the squire had said.

" ' He was home before the rain come, your honour,
anyhow," said the policeman.

" I did not think about it then; but I thought
about it the next day, and for many a day after that.
What a mercy it was that the rain had come on ! If
it had not been for that, how could I have cleared
myself ? Ah, it was all the lass's prayer.

" Well, the other man was taken, and both of them
pleaded guilty. The keeper did not die, but he was
maimed for life, and lost the sight of one eye ; and
that night ended in the transportation of the two
who had waited and called for me at the gate when
I was fast asleep in the hedge.

" It was a long time before I could do anything
else but thank God for the prayer of the dear lass

that had saved me. But whatever the fright of that night did for me, there was one medicine that did me powers of good, one joy on which my heart grew strong and glad again ; it was to see the roses coming back once more upon the lass's cheeks, and to see them beginning to grow upon the little lad's too. And they crept even outside the house, and began to grow about our door, as you may see them to this day, climbing right away up to the roof.

" So that New Year ended as well as it began, and better, too.

" And now, lads, the New Year is close upon us again. You can settle, by God's grace, what it is going to be. Grip your good thoughts and shape them while they are hot. Bend the New Year right whilst it is new. I wish you all a Happy New Year ; but a Happy New Year is a thing that takes more than wishing. Every man has got to beat that out on his own anvil, and to make it with his own arm. You can't begin it better than the way I began it five-and-thirty years ago—*sign the pledge and ask God to help you.*"

Then Old Nath lifted up his eyes, and a glad smile greeted a new comer who stood in the doorway.

" Here's mother to say that supper's ready. Eh, lass, I have been telling the chaps about you. Come on, Tommy, let's have done. And so, God bless you all."

Inside the Breakwater.

SOME time ago an incident occurred at Plymouth which produced a great deal of excitement, and of which the papers gave a very graphic account.

In a heavy gale of wind, a large steamer had become disabled off the Lizard Point. Two steamtugs came to her help, and managed to tow her nearly into the Plymouth Sound; but just as they got within two or three hundred yards of the Breakwater, the force of the gale became so great that they were unable to do anything more, and had to fling her off in the darkness of the night to shift for herself. In the midst of the furious storm they could not possibly help any further. The captain at once fired his signals of distress, let the anchors go, and hoped they might hold on until break of day.

But in such a gale and in such a place it was very doubtful if the cables would stand the strain; and as the tremendous seas swept over the ship, more than once the anchors actually began to drag. Then the tide went back and another peril appeared : the ship was in danger of being knocked to pieces on the rocky ledge of the Breakwater itself. As the morning dawned, the Hoe and the surrounding coast was covered by the people, who eagerly watched the perilous position. There against the stormy black sky was the steamer, the flag of distress fluttering in the angry winds ; now hidden in the great seas that broke over her, then flung up into dreadful clearness on some tremendous wave ; then straining at the cables, her frightened passengers and crew staring death in the face. So *outside* the Breakwater.

But *inside* the Breakwater the ships lay calmly

anchored under its shelter. The little fisher lad slept gently rocked on the sea, all ignorant of the peril that was so near him. Inside all was calm and safe.

Such was the difference that day, as to which side of the Breakwater a ship was. But there is a contrast immensely greater than that. Death comes to all men some time; and he could be met in many a worse fashion than bravely facing him as our noble sailors do in every gale that blows about our coasts. In such matters, even safety and peril is but a difference for a little while.

But there is a difference that is eternal. There is an *outside* that means everlasting death—an *inside* that means everlasting life.

And that peril of the steamer is past. She got safely into harbour, and now it is all a distant and half-forgotten thing. But this contrast is now and here. A difference that comes right home to us. We do not hear of it only. We are more than on-lookers at it. *We* are on one side of the Breakwater or the other—outside in storm and peril; or inside in the blessed shelter and safety. And yet can we be mad enough to turn from it as of no interest to us? When some ship has been in danger, driven toward the coast by a storm, I have seen men roused to any effort, flinging prudence to the winds in their eagerness to help; and as the peril has increased they have rushed, risking their own lives on behalf of those in danger. And can we think of this, *our own peril*, with little earnestness and concern ? Let us pray to God for His Holy Spirit to take away this strange and dreadful blindness.

Our only safety and peace is inside the Break-water.

Look at the stormy outside.—" There is no peace, saith the Lord, unto the wicked." How can there be ? God the Most High is the great Creator of all things—their King and Lord. And He has made us and all things for this one end—*to serve Him*. Everything in us and about us is exactly fitted to this end, to find its only true life and Blessedness in serving Him. The dull earth He has shaped after His will. The stars He controls in their courses. The seasons He directs in their order. The great wild seas are held in His hand, they ebb and flow exactly as He bids them. The animals He governs by the instinct He has given them. And to us, as having will and intelligence, He gives His Holy Word and Commandments. And all things—earth and star and sea, and living things about us, and men and angels—are blest as they do His will. " I am the Lord thy God," He saith to every one of us ; " Thou shalt love the Lord thy God with all thine heart." Now when a man goes against God, what peace can there be for him ? He is out of joint with all things. The great end and purpose of all things beats against him. Full of unrest and weariness, all living things seem happy compared with him.

Peace?—What peace can there be when the laws of the great Creator are set aside? When the King tracks the rebel at every step, and reads all the guilty secrets in his heart, and every hour brings nearer the terrible reckoning day, how can such an one be at peace?

The wicked man is at strife with himself.—Man is made for God, and he quickly finds out that he is too great to be satisfied with anything less. The soul that is great enough for God can never be filled by a round of eating and drinking and working and sleeping, or by any knowledge or honour or wealth. You cannot fill the heart with pleasures and hollow vanities. The whole world might belong to one man and yet he should cry from his heart, " I perish with hunger ! " Every now and then the forgotten and perishing spirit of the man speaks out against the dreadful emptiness within, and sends forth its great longing for some true, full, abiding blessedness. Thank God! there is too much of us,—blind, blundering fools though we be,—there is too much of us to be filled and satisfied with anything less than God Himself. These hungry clamours of the soul can be quieted only in knowing Him and serving Him. There is no rest but in Him. Then only can

the soul cast anchor in any calm shelter,—when we
have found the safety of His love.

There is no peace, saith the Lord, unto the wicked.
—Every man finds it so. What peace can there be
when poor weary Hope goes circling over the dreary
earth, and can find no sure resting-place for the sole
of her foot ? What peace can there be when beggary,.
bankruptcy, ruin stare him in the face ; the man
himself deathless, and yet the only possessions he
has slipping daily out of his hand as the moments
pass ? How can there be peace when every now and
then conscience wakes up and mutters fiercely of the
folly and the emptiness of life without God ? when
memory keeps uncomfortably whispering of the
wasted years, and fear keeps pointing us on to where
the thunder-clouds gather black and threatening ?
It is true, miserably true—" *there is no peace unto the
wicked.*"

And to the man who is without God *life itself is a
storm and turmoil.* God is the wise and gracious
Father ordering all things for our training. The
thousand circumstances and events of every day are
to teach and correct and develop us ; to make true
men of us. As we seek to make men of our children,
by the daily lessons at school, so God seeks to pre-
pare us for higher service, and would make us ready
to be trusted with greater gifts. But what is life to
a man who has no God ? No Father's hand controls

it, no loving wisdom orders it.   The hindrances and
annoyances, the losses and pain and sorrow, are just
wild storms that beat upon him pitilessly.   Life itself is a sea, pleasant enough in the summer-time;
but where dreadful storms burst and angry waves
sweep and toss in lawless fury, and there is no
breakwater, no harbour, no anchorage,—" There is
no peace, saith the Lord, unto the wicked."   So is it
outside.

.   .   .   .   .   .

Now let us look inside the Breakwater.—The wild
winds are hushed; the waves have ceased to thunder
and threaten.   The anchor holds without a strain at
the cable.   There is no peril.   It is as if the Lord had
spoken His " Peace be still"; and there is a great
calm where the ship is gently rocked on the bosom of
the deep.

See well what makes this safety.   Against fierce
waves and furious winds there rises the Breakwater.
The great seas that come sweeping on madly are
dashed against it into harmless spray, and fall back
spent and powerless.   The storm comes howling over
the tumbling billows and hurls itself against the
Breakwater, but it cannot leap over on its prey:
there, within its kindly shelter, all is calm.   It is the
wondrous truth of our salvation. *He is our peace.*
The Man is an Hiding-Place.   " All Thy waves and
Thy billows are gone over Me," is spoken concerning

Him. Upon Him the destroying tempest breaks, that
we may be sheltered and safe. " The chastisement
of our peace was upon Him ; and with His stripes we
are healed." Hiding in Him, safe shelter is ours from
the angriest storms that rage. *We have peace with
God through our Lord Jesus Christ.* " Who is he
that condemneth ? " In heaven or earth or hell, there
is no voice that can be lifted against him who hides
for refuge in this Rock of ages. There all fear
is quieted. Hope has found a sure and blessed
Rest. Over all the past God has breathed the hush
of His forgiveness, and all the future is bright with
the glow of heaven's sunny distance. Peace is within and peace around. Ah, there is blessed shelter
for the storm-tossed inside the Breakwater !

But look again upon the wild storm and the ship
in peril. *How is she to get within its safety ?* It is
no use for her to begin to boast of herself, of her
three thousand tonnage, or that she is A1 at Lloyd's,
or of the gales she has weathered, that she has crossed
the Atlantic a score of times, and been round the
world—*help must come to her*, or she will go down.
And for crew, in addition to her own picked men, she
has on board thirty of Her Majesty's naval officers
who happened to be returning from special naviga-
tion in the Chinese seas. All her strength and size,
and all the skill of her crew will avail her nothing
now. *She is the wrong side of the Breakwater.*

What she is or what she is not counts for little. She must go to pieces unless they can send her help.

"Ah," you say, "if I were not so weak, or if I were only more like such a one; if I were only more in earnest or had more faith, I should do then." No; your safety is not in your strength, or your goodness, or your earnestness, or in anything else. *It is in Him Who comes to help, and in Him alone.*

And the disabled steamer can do nothing for herself.—It is no good to trim the sails or put the helm about. All she can do is to fling up the signals of distress and to fire the cannon for help. Ah, how often, when we find the sorry plight and peril that we are in, we spend all our time in trying to right ourselves! Let us learn this lesson—we are past helping ourselves. "I will try," or "we must do our best, you know," just means nothing at all in seeking salvation. We can do nothing but send up the signal of distress. Let the cry of our hearts go up into the ears of the Lord, "*God be merciful to me a sinner!*"

Look once more at the disabled steamer, flung on the wild seas outside the Breakwater there. *She must get out of this peril, or all will be lost.* If she stays where she is, she must be knocked to pieces on the rocks. Every minute makes her position one of greater danger, and her escape more difficult. Do not let them stay a moment. Keep the danger-

signals flying—let the cannon boom. Give them no
rest within there. Let them know that it is urgent,
and if they are coming to help, they must come
quickly.

Ah! what peril is ours until we have found the
blessed way inside the Breakwater! The tide of life
is running out swiftly, and we are held on by the
brittle thread that may snap at any moment. And
then the awful perishing, going down into death with
black despair! And from the Judgment-Seat of God
the dreadful sentence waits for those who have re-
jected the offers of His mercy. There is no peace
for the wicked on there. Oh, the terrible storm that
shall sweep us from His presence, when, with unutter-
able grief, the Righteous Judge shall speak the words
of our condemnation!

Oh! the blessedness of the rest and peace into
which the righteous shall come when He shall say,
" Come, ye blessed of My Father, inherit the kingdom prepared for you from the foundation of the
world."

If the crew are to be saved, *they must just receive
the help that is brought to them, and keep fast hold of
it.*—Out come the Government steamers to the
rescue. The men of the life-boat carry the royal
cable with its scarlet thread, and bid them make it
fast. Think what folly it would be for them to throw
it angrily away! or to say that they thought it was

not meant for them! or to tell their helpers to go away now, and that they would decide to-morrow! or to say that their case is past help! And shall any man trifle with the offer of salvation in that way? Here, brother, *here* NOW is the Saviour's message to you, a cable that has never snapt with any strain, that has led thousands out of peril inside the breakwater,—*Whosoever believeth in Him shall not perish, but have eternal life.* Take hold of the Word. Trust yourself to Him. The Blessed Captain of our salvation can bring you safely into the Haven of Rest.

And now the cable is made fast—the steamers put forth their strength. But the disabled vessel will not stir. What is it? Why there, down through the boiling seas and right down to the rocks, gripping them tightly, are the anchors. *They must go.* What if the captain should hesitate, should begin to count the cost of them, and to haggle about giving them up! Ah, many a man is lost because he will not let go the anchor! Some secret sin holds him; something or other that he holds too dear to give it up. In vain all the signals of distress. In vain all the booming of the guns. In vain all the help that comes, and the efforts of brave men to save them. If you *will* not part with the thing that hinders, you must let go the rope of His mercy. But He is come to loose us from our sins. Our hands are numbed and strengthless to break the chains; but He brings the help we need. His very name is JESUS, Who saves us from our sins.

Then speedily there came the safety.—Not in vain was rocket and cannon and signal of distress. A hundred men came out with eager hands, and in spite of furious winds and thundering seas they brought the steamer out of her danger, nor left her until she lay all calmly sheltered within the safety of the Breakwater.

Our cry for help can never be in vain. The Blessed Lord is ever waiting to help us, and comes forth swiftly for our salvation. Through all the threatening hindrances, and in spite of all our helplessness, He brings us safe into the Blessed Haven of His salvation, where is eternal peace and safety. *" He is able to save them to the uttermost that come unto God by Him."*

Dick Croggan's Redemption.

CHAPTER I.

WHICH CONCERNS A BIRTH.

Poor little Dick! If ever heredity and environment were to be blamed, it was in his case. His father was a drunken sailor, who hailed from the East End of London. The only service he ever rendered his wife was that he took himself off for a three months' voyage, at least three times in the year, and went followed by a hearty wish on the part of his family that he might never come home again. This courtesy he repaid with interest by returning at the most inconvenient times possible, if indeed it were possible for his coming to have any degrees of inconvenience about it. His stay was determined by the time it took to turn his pay into liquor, to be duly consumed by himself and his mates. Meanwhile Mrs. Croggan, his wife, had to keep herself and her sticks of furniture together as best she could by odd jobs of charing at some city office—a poor slatternly

creature, soured and bittered by her hard lot, driven
by the colourless and cheerless life she lived to find
an occasional inspiration in gin.   The street in which
she dwelt was one of the grimiest in the parish of
St. George's, and the one room which she called her
home was the very poorest and wretchedest in the
street ; and that indeed was saying a very great
deal.

Here, then, it was that little Dick first saw the
light, or as much of it as could find its way through
the patched and dirty back window of Mrs. Croggan's
den.   The little stranger was not blest at his coming,
still less blest was he when he ceased to be a stranger.
Others had come before him—boys and girls—but,
after a good look round, had retired from a condition
of things in which there was so little inducement to
remain ; and perhaps it was expected that Dick
would show a similar discretion.   But Dick had
come to stay.   How he managed it was a mystery
—living anywhere but at home all day, and, when
his father was at sea, sharing at night the room with
his mother and an occasional lodger—certain it is
that Dick grew up to be a little white-faced fellow
of seven.   A life thus far without a touch of love,
without a ray of hope, with scarcely a gleam of gladness ; a life in which the consciousness was mostly
one of hunger and cold ; his only education a sturdy
defiance of his circumstances and of the world

generally—a beast of prey, he could bite and scratch, and kick and fight, or run away, as well as any beast of prey about him.

Now it was that there came into little Dick's life a gladness like the springing of flowers, and the singing of birds, when the winter is over and gone. It was from an unlikely source that there came this joy. Poor Mrs. Croggan had to snatch a few be-grudged moments from the everlasting round of charing to give birth to another baby. As soon as this event was accomplished, as the only chance of keeping her employment poor Mrs. Croggan had to be at work again, whilst little Dick was at once installed as mother and nurse to the new-comer. Is it not safe to say that all the freaks of nature repeat themselves in human relationships? The cuckoo's egg dropped in the hedge-sparrow's nest has its counterpart amongst us men and women. Only by some such principle was it possible indeed that so sweet a bit of mortality as this baby could have found its way from some heaven to such a place as Mrs. Croggan lived in. Specially was it a mystery when one thinks that there were dainty ladies in the land ready to give their very lives for such a treasure, and their lords with great estates waiting eagerly and all in vain for some such little soul to come and claim them. With such openings awaiting it else-where, we wonder that it should have settled here, unless indeed it were from sheer pity for poor little Dick.

But Dick himself never stayed for a moment to discuss the mystery of the coming. All he did at once and henceforth was to give himself up to the care of the baby. You turned out of the main road through a long and narrow street, past a row of dirty houses, and under a strip of sky that was stained and spotted with foul smoke. You saw big, brazen-faced women in the doorways, noisily talking, whilst crowds of dirty children quarrelled on the pavement. You saw bruised faces, with many varieties of black eye, recent or remote. Then amidst all this, you came upon little Dick, capless and shoeless, a bit of string having to hitch up the tattered trousers that clad, even if they did not conceal, his legs ; and in his arms he carried the baby, wrapped in a ragged shawl which had been saved for this purpose only because it was worth nothing at the pawnshop. All day long Dick sang to the baby ; he chirruped to it ; he had somehow to see to its feeding as well as to his own, and managed it wonderfully well, considering the raw material he had to deal with, and the little of it there was. And not by day only had Dick this care. When the father was at home in one of his drunken bouts, Dick would take the baby out of harm's way, and safe in some sheltered nook he sat with his ragged jacket wrapped round it to screen it from the rain or cold winds.

Neither of the children had ever been christened, but names came somehow—it was difficult sometimes to tell how. In this case the father knew the baby only as "the kid." With the mother it was "she." The neighbours knew it as "Mrs. Croggan's baby." But Dick had his own name for her, and he always called her "Beauty." Never was knight truer to his lady love, or braver in her defence than was little Dick. And never did love bring with it a more tender grace or sweeter gentleness than was inspired in this little fellow's heart. Dick dreamed of the life that he would live for her sake; of the monsters he would slay, in which the drink dragon stood out most terrible; of the noble things he would do; and castles as fair and stately as ever poet imagined rose in lofty grandeur as the little fellow planned his life with Beauty as the centre of it all.

CHAPTER II.

WHICH CONCERNS A DEATH.

THREE years had passed, and Beauty had grown more beautiful than ever. Not in little Dick's eyes only might this child have been beautiful; but the mother had no time and but seldom the temper to see in it much less than a burden ; and the father cursed the little brat as altogether in the way. But as the days went by not less but more intense was the bond between these two. Dick went along with the little one toddling at his side, or sat whilst the baby lay on his knees, laughing merrily, and with her arms about Dick's neck she rode half the day, borne from one shop window to another to feast on the treasures within.

It was in the depths of dull November when Mr. Croggan returned and proceeded to squander the earnings of his last voyage. It was a bitter night. The wild winds swept along the street, striking to the very marrow ; the lad hugged to himself the life that was dearer than his own ; but hunger and cold had nearly done their work. Fairy godmother the little couple had none, save old Biddy M'Carthy, who sat at the corner of the street and sold tarts. Not much of the fairy was in her face, sodden and fiery as it was with gin, her short clay pipe mostly held upside down and turned to leeward so that the ashes might not fall on her stores. Fortunately, perhaps, the public inspector had never analyzed the contents of these wares.

Frank Buckland tells a story of an old woman with a terrible cough, who presented herself every week at St. George's Hospital, bringing her bottle to be refilled with the mixture as before. She praised the medicine, but never seemed to get better, and any proposed change was stoutly resisted. At length his suspicions were aroused, and he watched her. He found her selling tarts at Westminster Bridge, the pastry tough and leathery, so that the teeth should have enough for their money, and held like a dull black eye in the centre was a dab of this precious cough mixture, which she should have been taking every three hours in a table-spoonful of water.

But whatever the composition of Biddy's tarts, it is certain that to Dick and his little sister life would have been paradise if only these tarts would have lasted for ever. Biddy, won by the sight of their love and by the beauty of the child, was accustomed to give them one of these fancy dainties. It was always supposed to be shared, Dick taking his turn with the little one, but his lips only eagerly mumbled over it, and then he passed it back, like the cunning hypocrite that he was, and let his sister have it all. There were times when the drunken freaks of Mr. Croggan had driven Dick and his little charge to the shelter of Biddy's room for the night. But, alas, at this time Biddy was away. To the profession of tart-making she added that of monthly nursing—so-called—though the period of attendance was more generally limited to a week.

The child was ill, very ill; what was the matter

Dick did not know, only that the heavy little head
lay for hours upon his shoulder, and, when he stirred,
the drooping eyes and flushed face filled the lad with
anguish. " If Beauty were to die," he whispered—
and he could but bite his lip and rock the child to
and fro,. occasionally thrusting a dirty knuckle
vigorously into his eye. Dick had set himself to make
the child as comfortable as he could. The process of
going to bed was a very simple one. There was
neither change of clothing nor bed to lie on. Against
the wall the lad had set what things he could gather,
and carefully wrapped up his sister, and then lay
down himself with his arm about her, and so they
slept. The mother had gone with her husband to
share in the drunken festivities which celebrated his
return, and late at night they both came staggering
up the stairs. The door was burst open and the
father was stumbling on his way, when he caught his
foot against Dick. With a horrible oath he kicked
out as fiercely as he could. Dick sprang up much
hurt, and by the flickering light of the gas-lamp
outside he saw his father. Instantly he shrank
before him, expecting another blow, when he saw the
brute lift his foot to kick the sleeping child out of
his way. Like a tiger Dick sprang at his father with
all his might. Reeling as he was, it needed no great
strength to send him over, and beneath the lad's
fierce attack the father fell heavily on the floor.

Dick snatched up the child and made for tho stairs. With a volley of oaths the father rose and rushed at him. But he was too late. Dick was away; out into the street, into the bitter cold of the night he ran, never resting for a moment until he made sure that he was safe. Then, seated

in a doorway, he sheltered the child as best he could from the biting winds, although he

was himself numbed by the intense cold. " Dick,"
whispered the child, putting up her hand, and draw-
ing his face down to herself. " Dear Dick ! Kiss
me, Dick."

The poor lad bent down over the little face, and as
the tears filled his eyes he kissed her tenderly.

" 'Tis so cold, Dick," shivered the little one, and she
shrank in close beneath the sheltering jacket. So
passed an hour, the stillness broken by the strokes
of the church clock, and the far-off screams of some
drunken brawl. But no ear, no eyes had Dick for
anything but the child that lay breathing so heavily
in his arms.

"If only Biddy were at home," sighed Dick.
Presently the little one stirred again.

" Dick," came the little voice.

" Yes," said Dick, his heart almost too full to get
out the words.

" Let me kiss you, Dick." Again he bent down, and
the arms were clasped about his neck, the head nestled
on his shoulder, and the lips were pressed against his
cheek. Another hour had gone. Dick was afraid to
stir lest he should disturb the child. Then, suddenly
the arms let go their hold of him, and the head fell
back. The lad knew that the end was come. His
little Beauty was dead. Numbed and starved, feeling
that life had lost its all for him, he rose and crept back
to the room. He opened the door, and stepped over

the sleeping father. Nobody could do her any harm now. Dick laid the dead child down beside his parents, took one more look at the face, then turned and fled, and never set foot in the place again.

CHAPTER III.

WHICH CONCERNS A RESURRECTION.

THE days passed by—Dick scarcely knew how, and cared less. He lived like hundreds of lads have to live in London, picking up a few pence in the street, honestly or otherwise, as the case might be. He felt that now he had nothing to care for—nothing for which he should keep himself apart from the worst. It was not long before he got into some trouble, and was apprehended by the police, and sent by the magistrate to a reformatory. Here he grew only more hardened. Careless and defiant, he was often punished, until, suspected of an attempt to set the training-ship on fire, he was wrongly sentenced to a severe penalty of imprisonment. This, of course, left him only more embittered, and by the time he reached manhood he was a very Ishmaelite—his hand against every man and every

man's hand against him. Reckless, hardened,
brutal, no man was sunk lower or seemed more
hopeless. A civil word could scarcely pass his
lips. A scowl had settled on his face, and the dull,
stupid features were never brightened by a gleam of
good humour.

. . . . . .

Ten years had passed. The Royal Mail steamship
O—— was making her way homeward. Dick had
found a place on board as common seaman. Coarse,
foul-mouthed, stubborn, no favourite was he either
in the forecastle or anywhere else. Bo'sun and
quartermaster had as little to say to him as possible,
and said what they said as sharply as they could.

It was a lovely day. The sun gleamed and danced
on the deep blue of the Indian Ocean. The passengers sat under the awnings in luxurious laziness.
Trotting about the deck, going from one to another
with merry prattle, was a little maiden of some three
summers ; the pretty little face peeped from under
the big straw hat, and about it hung clusters of
golden curls. Breaking down the most rigid caste,
she went looking up to each with a smile, and asking
a hundred questions. It chanced that day that Dick
was busied about the fastening of a boat that hung
near the deck ; with one leg swung over the rail and
one hand grasping the iron above, he hung at the
side of the ship. On came the little one towards him,

her chubby hands thrust behind her back, and her bright eyes eagerly watching him.

"What is you called?" she asked presently.

"Dick," was the answer.

"Poor Dick," said the little child again as she watched him swaying over the side, "Mind you don't tumble, Dick."

Dick looked and sighed. Back again from across the years came the very image of his lost little one. The look, the tone, the manner, all reproduced her.

Poor Dick, indeed! With every word came memories that softened and saddened his heart as it had not been softened for many a day.

"Dick," the little one went on, "I'm coming up to help you."

All unnoticed the child had gone behind him, and began to climb the railings to get up to him. The chubby little hands had grasped the iron and climbed from one to another until she rested on the second bar from the top, then lifting up her hands towards him she cried, "Dick, I am coming up to you."

Dick turned, only to see the little figure balanced for a moment—then, before he could stoop to reach the uplifted hands, there came a swaying of the ship, and with a shriek the child was overboard. As everybody moved to the side they saw Dick leap from the boat into the sea, and in a minute he held the child safely in his arms. Before the steamer could be stopped they were far behind, but there was the little one clinging to Dick, whilst the golden curls were floating on the blue sea and the little face nestled against his own. To him all the lost years had come back again. It was his own " Beauty " that lay once again in his arms, and he was no more the hard and brutal man, but the tender-hearted little lad, and the dreams of deliverance were fulfilled. Quickly came the boat to their rescue, but still the little one clung to Dick, and still that strong arm pressed her to his heart.

" Dear Dick," whispered the child, nestling against him as the little one used to do long ago, and the lips kissed him. " Dear Dick——"

Amidst shouts and hurrahs they were received on board, but Dick shrank away from it all. A large sum of money was quickly collected, but this was resolutely refused. Dick's reward waited for him every day as he was sent for by the little queen, and as she climbed upon his knee, and put her arm about his neck and whispered, " Dear Dick."

So it was that the chubby little hand began to loosen bolts that were old and rusty, and which no force could break ; began to open doors that had been shut for years, and to let light from heaven into the dungeon. And thus awoke and lived again the great true love of long ago—for all true love is immortal and sleeps only, but can never die.

Dick's very face began to be as that of another man. Day by day there came a deepened tenderness ; another tone and manner ; and henceforth Dick Croggan lived in that goodly land of kindness, whither every little child is sent to lead us all, if we will but be led.

A Gift for You.

SOME time since, as I was stepping into the train at Newcastle, a gentleman came up to me and said he was going my way, and if I did not object he would take his seat in the same compartment, as he had been wanting to see me. I was very glad to have his company. He was good enough to say that he had met with a story a little while before which he thought might serve me. A friend of his, living some few miles from Newcastle, was walking along a railway siding going from the main line to a colliery, when he looked down upon a roughly-built cottage, and noticed that the daylight showed through the loose tiles on the roof. He wondered if anybody could be living in a place that appeared so cheerless, and, coming round to the front, he found an old woman and her grown-up daughter. At once he said within himself that he would see the place was made more comfortable before the winter came, and then hurried on his way. But the good purpose was forgotten, and he never thought of the place again until one morning some few weeks after he drew up

"Mine?" said his Lordship; "*Mine?*" taking the deed
and opening it again.

[*Page* 127.

I

his blind and looked out to find two or three inches
of snow on the ground. At once his heart smote
him for his forgetfulness. He had that day to go to
Newcastle, and it occurred to him that at any rate a
pair of blankets would do something towards adding
to the comfort of the couple. He reached his house
with the big brown-paper parcel, and thought he
would have the pleasure of taking them himself. As
he passed the window the old woman was looking out,
and he held up the parcel, thinking she would understand that he was bringing something for her. But
she only frowned angrily and shook her head. He
opened the door; when the old woman bade him angrily begone; she did not want to *buy* any of his
goods, she said, and slammed the door against him.
" Why," he said, " *she thinks I want to sell them!*
No wonder she is so vexed, needing them so badly.
I must make her understand that it is a gift." He
opened the door again and got in. More fiercely
than ever she bade him begone. He saw that she
was stone deaf, and that her daughter was not at
home. What could he do? To leave the parcel
would only be to have it flung after him in the snow.
" I will show her what it is," he said to himself;
" perhaps she will understand then," and he untied
the parcel.

But the sight of the warm blankets only made her
more conscious of her need and her poverty, and she

turned away indignantly.   " Why don't you go away ?
I have told you I don't want them."

What could he do ?   He took one out and held it
up full length and breadth, and smiled and nodded

his head, but it seemed only like the insinuating wiles of some resolute peddler, and aggravated her the more.

" Why don't you go away when I tell you ? " she cried.

Then yet another effort suggested itself. Taking the blanket, he threw it right round her and burst into a hearty laugh. Then the meaning of it all flashed upon her. Looking up, almost afraid to ask the question, she asked : " *For me ?* "

He nodded his head and smiled.

"*A gift?*" she asked again, her hope growing bolder. Again he nodded his head.

" *A gift for me !* " she repeated to herself. She stroked it with her hands and felt the warmth of it ; then laughed and cried for very joy ; she grasped his hands, and thanked him with all her heart, whilst the tears streamed down her wrinkled cheeks.

Alas that our blessed Master should have such trouble to force His gifts upon us ! Alas that we are so deaf, so blind to His great love !

He speaks to-day to you : *Come unto Me, all ye that labour and are heavy laden, and* I WILL GIVE YOU REST. Here is a gift *for you.*

Let us listen to the words. At the outset it is very needful for us to hear these words aright ; and that can only be by coming to Him Who spake them at the first. Dried fruits may keep something of their flavour, but they lose the bloom, and shape, and beauty; they lack all the surroundings of foliage and garden wealth, and the glory of the skies beneath which they grew. Alas! how shrivelled and hard is this great utterance as it falls from our lips. That which no man could ever have thought, any man may well hesitate to utter. Only the great Heart that held the world could have spoken these words; and only He can speak them still. Think of Him looking forth upon all the burdened and heavy-laden, conscious that in Him there is that which meets the want of the whole world. Many men in every age have clamoured fiercely for the world's heeding, and have cried aloud: " Come unto me, and I will give you happiness, honour, excitement, splendour, wealth, health." How much more perfect was His knowledge of the world's need Who bent over it and said: " *I will give you rest.*" It is good to think that once in the midst of men there stood One Who spake thus. But it is better still to think that He stands in *our* midst and speaks thus *now*. This " Come unto Me," implies a present and approachable Christ: Christ within reach of me and within my reach. Those eyes that search all secrets, so full of tenderest pity, look on thee and me, and as if there were no other to be helped He saith to us, *I will give you rest*. It shall avail us nothing to hear a thousand sermons about these words, no matter how splendid;

the blessedness is ours only as *we come to Him.* We cannot come in the wrong way if we do but come— with fearful step, groping in blindness, only coming, the gift is ours. At His feet these words fall from His lips like healing balm, like the great hush of His authority over the winds and waves. *Come unto Me*—blessed be God, it is not far to go. It is to set thought and heart upon Him, to look up saying, "Here am I, Lord—for Thou didst call me, and I am come." Strange, indeed, is it that this is ever the last thing we do—coming right away to Jesus. We go anywhere and to anything sooner than alone to Him! and yet nothing else can avail us. Salvation is too great a work for any short of the Lord Jesus Christ Himself; and the Saviour is too eager for our help to entrust it to other hands. *Come unto ME.*

.   .   .   .   .   .

I will—the music grows richer and sweeter with every note. Stay yourself upon that word. Venture your all for eternity upon it. It is fixed and unalterable. Now can we hold Him by this truth. Now is it no more a matter in which my Master hath any choice. By that "I will" He hath bound Himself, and bound Himself to me. I will *give.* It is wholly without condition. There is here nothing about learning of Him or taking His yoke: nothing even about repentance and faith and feeling.

But are they not needful?

Of course they are, and *because they are needful they shall be given with the gift.* My Master doth not cheat me by setting the gift on the pinnacle of the Temple, and promising it with much show of grace if I can but get it. Never, never. He gives repentance, faith, feeling—all that can make the gift most gracious and most complete His bounty delights to bestow.

And now do you ask, What is the rest? Well, different persons will set most stress upon different aspects of it, and the rest is fullest and completest where most of all the burden of life presses. To some it is above all else *rest from the mystery, the loneliness, the burden of life.* In Jesus Christ there is the revelation of a Love in which we delight. God's love is ours—the rest and blessedness as of a little wearied child that has found again the mother's arms and rests against her heart. God's great love underlies and commences as well as over-arches and completes every other gift that Christ gives to us. Life is, indeed, a burden of mystery. Here are we, so shaped by circumstances, and yet with such possibilities for good or evil within us; so hemmed in by the present, and yet with eternity lying about us; so dependent upon this world, and yet ever feeling its wretched insufficiency; at times longing to be holy, and yet with such temptations and impulses to evil; so weak, and yet with desires, ambitions, long-

ings that are infinite. Life is a thing of distractions.
Earth holds us, though Heaven beckons and Death
threatens, and we alternately hug the world and hate
it ; we sigh for Heaven, and then despise it ; we dread
Death, yet play with it. And Jesus Christ looks
forth pitifully upon us, and bids us come unto Him.
In Him life loses all its loneliness. With us everywhere and in everything there is an abiding Presence
—helpful, comforting, delivering. God is no more
only the great Creator afar off, but my Father,
stooping to take my hand, teaching me that I am
dear, unutterably dear to His heart ; that for me He
has most gracious and most glorious purposes ; and
all the way of life is but the path in which He is
leading me on to truer blessedness ; developing and
ennobling me. The feverish worry and over-eager-
ness of life fall from our shoulders as we rest in His
care. The fierce and hungry desires that went out
after the world are uplifted, and now find in Him their
satisfaction. There is deep, true, blessed rest in the
revelation of the Father.

Then out of this infinite love there comes the next
step in our rest. Behind us there is a past that we
cannot conceal ; that awful procession of deeds and
words and wishes ; and all the life's influence follow-
ing us. A past which cannot be left behind ; a
burden that grows each day. No skill, no desperate
effort can loosen the knots. In our midst there

standeth One Who saith; " Come unto Me, and I will give you rest." *How* we need not stay to understand, rejoicing in the fact that the Son of man hath power on earth to forgive sins. Blessed be God, there are thousands who do know what it is to come to Him! One touch of that Hand, and the burden is gone. Cast behind God's back ;—buried in the depth of the sea ;—remembered against us no more for ever ;—removed from us as far as the East is from the West,—this is ours in Christ Jesus. " Being justified by faith, we have peace with God through Jesus Christ our Lord." Think of the disciples tossed in the storm upon the lake, when the great waves surged about the little craft, hung over them in awful threatening, crouched to spring upon them again, and then leapt, roaring and hissing as if impatient for their prey. Before, behind, above, beneath, the cruel waters that gathered in their strength against them. Then suddenly He came, with outstretched Hand. *Be still*—and there was a great calm ; and the starry heaven looked down upon the sleeping sea. Think not that His Power and Love have spent themselves —nay indeed, no more than His sun has spent its light and heat. Open the ear of the heart ; He speaks now to you—*Come unto Me, all ye that labour and are heavy laden, and I will give you rest.*

And for the future, as from the past, He is our peace. Born of God, we are now of His family and household.

If children, then heirs; being trained and fitted for a high estate, until we are of age and enter upon our great inheritance. So do we stand. About us, the ceaseless, all-controlling love of God; behind us, a past in which all condemnation is for ever hushed; before us, growing nearer and clearer, the sunny distance of the Father's house. Believing, we have entered into rest.

But it is not enough to hear the words. WE MUST TAKE THE GIFT.

In the midddle of the last century there lived in the county of Somersetshire a good old baronet, who owned one of the largest and loveliest estates in all the west country. Without either wife or child or any near relative, he resolved to leave his property to the Earl of Chatham, whose noble devotion to the welfare of his country, and whose freedom from all selfish aims had kindled the squire's intense and enthusiastic admiration. So he sent for his solicitor, and had the deed drawn up in due form, directing that at his death his solicitor should proceed to London, and himself place the document in the earl's own hands, providing, at the same time, for the disposal of the estate in case his lordship should refuse to accept it.

Soon afterwards the baronet died, and the solicitor set out on horseback for London, with the precious deed safely stowed in his saddle-bags. In those days

London was a long way off. In those days, too, fashions travelled very slowly, if indeed they ever reached so far as that obscure little village in Somersetshire whence the lawyer came. So, as he jogged along the streets of London, men turned their heads to see this fresh-looking man from the country, in his dress of homespun. His manner, his dialect, all proclaimed him a stranger. What indeed could such an one as he have to do with the Earl of Chatham?

He speedily made his way to his lordship's house and knocked at the door. But getting in was another matter.

"I would see his lordship," said the solicitor. "Is he at home?"

The haughty servant-man gave him a withering glance from head to foot, and then, lifting his head scornfully, he said, "His lordship does not see every common person who happens to come to London."

The lawyer grew indignant. "He had better see me. If he does not, it will be a bad day's work for him—the worst he ever did," and he laid his hands on the documents.

"What insolence, indeed!" thought the high and mighty flunkey, wondering what things were coming to, when folks from the country talked like this! He was about to bid him begone about his business when, fortunately for the earl, some higher official happened to pass ; and he stopped to ask what the man wanted.

"I *must* see his lordship," said the lawyer. " I have come all the way from Somersetshire on purpose, and I am not going away until I do."

Here was a man who knew his own mind, at any rate, and spoke it, too, for all it was in a Somersetshire dialect. These countrymen were resolute fellows, though they did wear homespun, and it might be an easier thing to get him an interview with the earl than to get rid of him without it.

" Well, can you not send a message ? Of course he cannot see you personally," asked the official.

" But he *must*," said the solicitor. " My business with him is of the utmost importance. I cannot entrust it to anyone else. If he does not see me he will be very sorry for it some day."

" Well," was the reply, " I will see what can be done."

So he waited in the hall. After a long delay, he was passed from one to another until at last the message reached his lordship. Somebody from Somersetshire would speak with the earl on urgent business.

" What does he want with me ? " asked the earl, pressed with a thousand cares, and little willing to be hindered by some troublesome countryman interviewing him about some fancied grievance.

"He says, my lord, that he must see your lordship; he cannot entrust his business to a messenger."

"Well, well, I suppose I must give him a few minutes. I will see him."

At last the solicitor was ushered into his lordship's presence.

"What is your business?" asked the earl, eyeing the man curiously, and scarcely concealing his impatience.

The solicitor produced the deed, and, craving his lordship's indulgence, said he would proceed to read the document, which would explain itself. So he began hurrying through the old legal phraseology as rapidly as he could.

"What in the world has this to do with me?" said the earl to himself, wondering how much time he was going to waste in this fashion. "Why does he come troubling me with these parchments?" And then his thoughts were busied with matters which seemed a great deal more important.

There seemed no end to the unmeaning mumble of the "aforesaid," and the "hereby," and the rest of it. Was there no way of getting rid of this fellow? At last the lawyer ceased, and, folding the document, he placed it in his lordship's hand.

"That is my business, my lord."

"But what have I to do with it?" said the earl, half-angrily, thinking his visitor crazy.

"Why, my lord!" cried the solicitor, amazed. "Don't you understand? *Burton Pynsent is yours.* The mansion and the estate, and all its belongings!"

"*Mine?*" said his lordship. "*Mine?*" taking the deed and opening it again.

"*Yours*, my lord. And this is the will of Sir William Pynsent."

"And he has left it to *me?*"

"Every inch of it is yours, my lord."

"Really, this is *very* interesting, *very*. Pray be seated, my dear sir."

Again he turned to the deed. Again he went over it, word by word, with the lawyer.

"I did not understand. Really, I must apologize, my dear sir," and the earl grasped the hand of the solicitor warmly. "But I must send for her ladyship, and you must tell her of our good fortune."

The countess was summoned. She came in, looking first at the country gentleman, as if to say, "What can he want here?" and then at the vellum.

The tale was quickly repeated.

"*Really*," said the countess, "*this is most interesting*. And you have come up from Somersetshire to put this into his lordship's own hands?"

"I was to entrust it to no other," said the lawyer, bowing.

"How very good of you!"

And they sat together, asking a thousand questions about the property; and the vellum was read through again.

" Of course, you will be good enough to make your home with us during your stay in town," said both of them.

And the room was prepared at once; and the country gentleman was entertained as a prince, and from that day the good lawyer became their adviser and trusted friend.

It is a sad thing when men are so busy that they cannot stay to hear good news.—What that library door of his lordship would have shut out if, because he had so many things to think about, he should have roughly dismissed the messenger. Alas! how true is it with many of us! We cannot stay to listen to the story of the legacy which is ours. The love of God which should lighten and gladden all the life —the great salvation to which we are heirs through Jesus Christ, if we will but accept it—the heavenly mansion, the great estate of blessedness which is made over to us. Poor, when we might be so rich; burdened, when we might be so blest; fearful, when confidence and peace might fill the soul—shall we not be still and listen to the good tidings of great joy which is addressed to us, and meant for us, if we will but hear it?

Depend upon it, the earl and countess *were not content with hearing.* Think if these two had just been content *to come together once in the week*, and for an hour and a half had sat solemnly in the library, with the household, listening to the mumbled phrases of the deed; his lordship dozing over it, and her ladyship trying not to think about her bibs and tuckers and furbelows. Why, everybody would have called them mad! They heard, but they were not content with hearing. They began at once to take possession of their property. The estate was *claimed* as their own; the house was lived in; the beauties were enjoyed; the rents were taken; the produce was turned to account.

To hear of great good is no good at all—worse than nothing, if that be all. That which is offered, let us accept; that which is promised, let us claim; let us go up and possess the good land, the land of peace and gladness which is made over to us. *Take heed how ye hear.*

. . . . . .

I heard a good story the other day of a poor old woman in Scotland whose son had gone abroad, and got on well. He wrote to the widowed mother to tell her with great joy that now she need not trouble any more, that as long as she lived he would send her the money for her rent. She was overjoyed, and carefully put his letters in an old broken teapot on the dresser;

K

and almost every night took them out and read them
with eyes filled with tears of joy.   But day after day
the time drew nearer for the payment of the rent,
and sweet as these words of her son were, still it

took more than pleasant words to satisfy the landlord.   At first she was angry with herself for the fears
that whispered within her.   Her son had promised
and promised again in every letter he wrote.   But

what of the promises if the money did not come!
At last the rent-day came. Surely the postman to-
day would bring the money. It was just like her
son to calculate so exactly and to send it just when
it was due. No! the postman went his way, and
there was nothing for her. The old soul tried to
keep up; there was some delay somewhere, but it
was all right, *to-morrow* would explain it all, and the
landlord could wait till to-morrow. But alas! many
to-morrows went by, and at last the landlord could
wait no longer. *The money must be paid—or she
must go.*

Once more she put on her spectacles and went
through the letters. There it was as plain as plain
could be. What could it mean? Oh, if he only
knew that to-morrow her little all would be sold for
rent!

Now it chanced that a friend, hearing of her
trouble, came in to see her.

" I thought your son promised to pay the rent?"
said the friend.

" He did!" said the old lady, shaking her head
very mournfully, " he did; and I can't think why he
isn't as good as his word."

" Will you let me see the letters?" said the friend.

" Yes," said the old woman, and she took down the
broken teapot from the dresser and fetched them
out.

The friend read them through. "Was there nothing in this letter?"

"Yes," said the old woman; "there was a strip of paper: some advertisement or something, *but no money.*"

"Where is it?" urged the friend. There it was, in the depths of the teapot. "*Why, it is a post-office order!*" said the friend; "more than enough to pay the rent."

Away they went to the post-office. There was some difficulty at first. The time had passed, but after a while the matter was explained. *The order was cashed;* and the old soul's trouble was at an end.

.   .   .   .   .   .

These texts of Scripture are not sweet words only to be read and treasured; they are blessed promises that we are to claim, to turn to account, to have for ourselves and for our own now and here. Take the word and claim its fulfilment right boldly. *Come unto Me, and I will give you rest.*

> I heard the voice of Jesus say,
>   "Come unto Me and rest;
> Lay down, thou weary one, lay down
>   Thy head upon my breast:"
> I came to Jesus as I was,
>   Weary and worn and sad ;
> I found in Him a resting-place,
>   And He has made me glad. ,

I heard the voice of Jesus say,
　" Behold, I freely give
The living water, thirsty one,
　Stoop down, and drink, and live ; "
I came to Jesus, and I drank
　Of that life-giving stream ;
My thirst was quenched, my soul revived,
　And now I live in Him.

I heard the voice of Jesus say,
　" I am this dark world's light ;
Look unto Me, thy morn shall rise,
　And all thy day be bright : "
I looked to Jesus, and I found
　In Him my Star, my Sun ;
And in that light of life I'll walk
　Till travelling days are done.

It was all through the Foot-and-Mouth Disease.

SOME years ago I lived in a remote part of the country. I had under my care a number of little outlying chapels, in which I held a fortnightly service on the week-night, and an occasional service on Sunday. The congregations that gathered were wholly agricultural, bringing with them the smell of a field that the Lord had blessed; and greatly delighted me by their simplicity and heartiness. Of these little country places there was one so remote and so insignificant that I very seldom got to it. It was miles from everywhere, and you wondered how it found its way there at all. Thus it was that because it was so hard to get at, and so small when you got there, it was compelled to be content with a service once a month, where more ambitious places demanded a visit once a fortnight. It was only the market-town itself that was bold enough to expect a service every week.

It took you a long time to get to the village of Trelaske, partly because it was so far off, but mostly

because the roads were so bad and the hills were so
steep. Uphill and down until you turned off the
high road and plunged into the deep ruts of winding
lanes, the sheltered hedge a very bank of soft
mosses and nodding ferns, crowned in the spring with
daffodils and starred with primroses; and later, gay
with foxglove and trailing honeysuckle—by day.
By night pitch-dark, a darkness that was felt in
thumpings and heavings and all kinds of joltings.

You came at last to the low little building in
which the service was held—the chapel with school-
room attached. Not a house was near it, except
that far up the lane you heard the ringing music of
the blacksmith's shop, and the blaze of ruddy light
streamed out to greet you with a cheery welcome.

Thither came the tribes to worship, mostly old
men and old women—for the young folks went into
the towns and stayed there. But whatever else
they found in the towns, they could not find faces
like these—so honest, so simple, and so contented.
The placid life they lived seemed to proclaim itself
in the round face, in the easy-going gait, and the
leisurely, kindly tones. There came old men in
orthodox black coats, with bulging pockets at the
side, their black tie mostly without a collar, but the
round, ruddy face set off by a white fringe of whisker
—too much hair about the face is still considered
worldly in out-of-the-world places. They met and

walked in front, whilst the dear old motherly
women came on behind—their faces full of cheery
contentment, looking out from black bonnets that
were made for shelter as well as for show, and the
skirts of the Sunday dress gathered carefully up,
whilst they picked their way as well as they could
along the muddy lane. As you drove on, you kept
coming upon such little groups, now leaping down
into the deep lane from unexpected stiles, almost
hidden by thick growth of bush and tree, or coming
out of some gateway. Here lingered still a sweet
leisureliness and simplicity which railways and
newspapers and hourly postmen have scared away
from most places.

The hero of my story lives at the farmhouse a
quarter of a mile farther on. There we have to put
up the trap, and they are expecting us to take a
cup of tea before the service. As we turn the corner,
we catch sight of the good farmer waiting for us at
the gate.

"How are 'e, then, sir? Glad to see 'e," is the
greeting; and the grip of the hand gives a force to
his words that is very emphatic. A man of middle
size was Farmer Venning as to height, but well-
rounded altogether; a face ruddy with good health
and much fresh air, altogether a man with whom
things went well and easily. We leave the trap in
the farmer's hands, and turn in, to find the good

wife and daughter waiting at the tea-table. The "splits" have been baked on purpose, and the glass dish with yellow clotted cream has been filled for our coming.

Farmer Venning was almost everybody and everything at the little chapel. He loved the place, and saw to it for every service, Sunday and week-day. Whatever wanted doing, he was always the man to do it. Nobody rejoiced more than he did when things prospered there, and nobody fretted more when things went badly. But—there was a but, a great big solid but—Farmer Venning's interest began and ended in the material prosperity of the place. As for anything further, that was left to the others, of whom all were willing, but scarcely one was able to render much service. A man who might have done so much good if he had thrown himself heart and soul into the work, it was difficult to let him stay where he was; and yet it was impossible to move him.

"Now, Farmer Venning," one would say to him, "why not become altogether a man of God? You hear the truth and enjoy it, and yet you do not surrender yourself to it. Why not do your duty? Give yourself right up to the claims of the Lord Jesus Christ, and serve Him. There is no one who could do so much good as you could, if you were only an out-and-out Christian."

But Farmer Venning shook his head, and said good-humouredly, "No, I don't see that I need be any better than I am. I don't want to boast, and I don't care to talk about it, but seeming to me I am so good as they that do set up to be religious. I try to do my duty, and I don't see what more anybody can want. Of course, everybody do make a slip now and then ; but I do not think that God is going to take notice of every little failing. I mean right enough, and I do so right as other people do, too."

There he stuck. Always willing to talk good-humouredly about it, yet the conversation always left him where it began. Sometimes he shyly added, "If some of your religious folks was a bit more like me, I shouldn't be sorry." And he looked across at some worker of the church who was somewhat too heavenly-minded to pay his debts very promptly. Such was Farmer Venning.'

.   .   .   .   .   .

I had left the neighbourhood for some years, when, happening to visit the principal town for some service, there to my astonishment I saw my old friend Venning, genial and hearty as he always was ; yet I fancied I saw another light in his face, and it was evident from his coming to attend the service and from the prominent part he took in it, that there was a change in the man.

"There's Venning," I whispered to my friend as we sat at a preliminary tea-meeting.

"Yes," said he.

"But I am astonished to see him here," I said. "He never used to come to this sort of thing, and I never saw him anywhere but at Trelaske."

"Haven't you heard the story of what happened to him? I must tell you about it."

Later that night when the service was over, and we gathered about the fire, "Now," said I, "do let me hear all about my old friend Venning."

"Well," my friend began, it was all through the foot-and-mouth disease."

"Did he get it, then?" I asked.

"No; neither he nor his cattle, for that matter. But it was in this way. You see his farm lies on either side of the little stream which divides the two counties."

"Yes," said I; "I remember it well. I have once or twice enjoyed an hour's fly-fishing in that stream."

"Well, when the foot-and-mouth disease broke out, orders were issued everywhere that no cattle were to be driven from one county to another. Directions were issued to the police everywhere to see that it was strictly obeyed; and a heavy penalty was attached to any offence against the law in this respect.

" Now our friend Venning had two or three cows that were grazing in a field on this side of the stream. The policeman passed in the early morning and saw them there. But during the day the farmer came out, and thinking a change of pasture would be good for the cows, he drove them across the field to the other side.

" As the policeman returned from his round, he caught sight of what had happened. The cows plainly enough were gone from this side ; and plainly enough they were peacefully grazing on the other side of the stream. Certainly Mr. Venning had broken the letter of the law, whatever the spirit of it might be. Probably the letter was what the policeman understood best ; at any rate it was most easily read. Big with the importance of the occasion, he made his way to the farmhouse, and inquired for Mr. Venning.

" Forth came the farmer without the least suspicion that there was anything wrong, and greeted the policeman with a cheery good evening—a greeting which the policeman scarcely returned.

" ' Be they your cows over there to the other side of the stream ? '

" ' Of course they are,' said Venning, wondering whatever the policeman had to do with his cows.

" ' And this morning they was *this* side of the stream, I b'lieve ? '

Farmer Venning turned his back upon all, and set out
with the policeman.

[*Page* 146.

" ' Certainly.'

" ' And you drove them across ? '

" ' Yes, I drove them across,' said the farmer, laughing at the solemnity of the cross-examination.

" ' 'Tisn't no laughing matter,' said the policeman, feeling himself trifled with.

" ' What isn't ? ' said Venning.

" ' Why, this here. *You've a been and gone and d.ove your cows right through a hact of Parliament ; '* and the policeman drew himself up, as if he were the embodiment of that law which the farmer had defied. ·

" ' Nonsense,' said Venning, a little more seriously, ' I drove my cows from one field to another.'

" ' You've—a—drove—your—cows—from—one— county—to—another,' repeated the policeman, with a pause between each word. ' And that do mean money, or prison.'

" ' But you are not going to make a fuss about that, surely.' The farmer was evidently growing frightened as to how much might be made of it.

" ' I don't know about a fuss. I be going to tell the magistrate.'

" ' Going to tell the magistrate that I drove my cows from one field to another ! Ridiculous ! '

" ' No ; I be going to tell him that you drove your cows *from one county to another,*' persisted the policeman. ' Of course if you can explain it to the magistrate, it will be all right; and if you can't, it be all wrong.'

" 'But a little thing like that! ' pleaded Venning.

" 'Yes, but a little thing like that is a big thing when it do break the law,' replied the policeman, tightening his lips and nodding his head.

Venning was silenced. The matter might mean a good deal more than he thought at first. For a moment he stood looking down on the ground loosening a stone with his foot. Then he turned to the policeman and asked, ' What had I better do, then ?'

" ' Well,' said the policeman, as if now the offender were coming to reason, 'I be going to the magistrate's. If you like to come 'long with me to his honour and tell him all about it, you can hear what he do say.'

" Venning was quite unwilling to admit to himself that the matter was of such importance as this seemed to make it; and yet if the policeman was going to say anything about it, certainly it would be better for the farmer to be there to explain how it happened. There was no help for it.

" ' Well, I suppose I had better go too,' said he at last, and they started together.

" They passed out through the little garden-gate and stood on the rising ground looking over the farm. The very quietness and beauty of the scene seemed to make the farmer more conscious of his trouble.

There were the cows coming down the lane, placidly, as if nothing had happened. They little knew what mischief they had caused, and who indeed knew what might come of it?

"The peaceful sky, flushed with sunset hues, made the presence of a policeman an offence. The thrush piped his evening hymn almost reprovingly at such an intruder; and deepening the peace, there came across the valley faintly the cawing of the rooks as they settled in the trees about the magistrate's house. No other sounds were there but the voices of the milkmaids as they called to 'Blossom' or 'Cherry' to come and take her turn to be milked.

"With a sigh, Farmer Venning turned his back upon all and set out with the policeman. What a thing, to be sure—and he had always prided himself that he did his duty! Presently they reached two or three cottages that made up the village of Trelaske. Out ran the wondering little lads and maidens, and stood stock still in the middle of the road, sturdy legs planted widely, and they looked up staring open-mouthed, until there came a burst of astonishment : ' Why, 'tes Farmer Venning.' And the women, hearing somebody passing, must needs come to the doorway to see who it could be, since there was so little to be seen. They began to curtsey a good-evening, but then seemed to break it off doubtfully. ' Mr. Venning goin' with the p'liceman,

L

and lookin' like as if he had somethin' 'pon his mind, too,' said each to herself, as she turned back wondering.

"At last Farmer Venning broke the silence. 'This here law is a terrible thing, when anybody do come to think about it.'

"The policeman was somewhat conciliated by the remark; it recognized the importance of the man who had to do with the handling of this terrible force, and therefore shared somewhat in its terribleness. He nodded his head and drew up his breath into a hissing assent, as if he must not be too ready to agree with any man who had set this terrible law at defiance. But the silence must not seem to be indifference. He stopped, and, looking at Farmer Venning, said solemnly, ' *'Tis the terriblest thing there is, if you do think about it, is the law.'*

"So they stood for a moment or two, and then went on again. But the solemnity of the utterance pulled the speaker up again, and once more he stopped to enforce his opinion on the subject. ''Tes a thing I do think a deal about,' said the policeman, 'when I be wandering up and down the roads, and nothing much for to do but to meditate 'pon things.'

"The tone of the policeman became quite cheerful. It was a relief to have somebody to listen to thoughts that the rural constable had spoken to himself half aloud, until they had got quite rolled and rounded into shape, like pebbles swept to and fro by the tides. It did not occur to him that the words which he uttered so jauntily were as swords and spears to Farmer Venning.

" 'Iss, a terrible thing is the law, and for good reasons, too. If you do come for to think about it, 'tis the law that do hold things together.'

" Farmer Venning looked inquiringly, slightly bewildered by the policeman's philosophy.

" 'You see,' the policeman explained, ' 'tis something like this here. You know in this here world that you can see there be something that do make things hold together an' keep them in their place— roads, and trees, and houses, and fields, and hills, and everything. Now if a man could put his hand 'pon something that would make these here things all fly to pieces like clouds of dust, that would be terrible, wouldn't it ? '

" ' It would be sure 'nough,' said the farmer.

" ' Now this here law is like that—it do keep things together, and keep 'em in their places. 'Tis no good saying *you ought* if you can't say *you must*, and you can't say *you must* if there bain't no law at your back. Things that is more than fields, and roads, and houses, would all fall to pieces if you tookt away the law. You couldn't never be safe, and you couldn't never be sure, if 'twasn't for the law. The law do give a man something for to stand 'pon—and

marketing, and marrying, and everything would all
fall to pieces if it wasn't for the law that do keep
folks to their duty and their rights. A terrible thing
is the law!'

"So Farmer Venning thought, a terrible thing indeed. A grim and solid thing which, if you fall
upon it, breaks you to pieces, and if it falls upon you,
grinds you to powder.

"'Why, if you do come for to think upon it, 'tes
everything, is the law;' and the policeman
tightened his lips, and nodded his head over his
black leather collar. There was no going beyond
that.

"They went on together in silence, and then the
policeman stopped again, as if there were another
side of the argument, and it was but fair that it
should be duly set forth—his mind so much taken
up with the subject that he quite forgot the unhappy
farmer.

"'Of course it do all depend which side of the law
you be. If you are 'pon the right side of the law
you've got everything for 'e, everything—the p'lice,
and the magistrates, and the judges, and the jails,
and the army and navy, and both Houses of
Parliament, and the Queen herself, is all for you
when you be 'pon the right side of the law.'

"'Umph!' grunted the farmer.

"'But if you be the wrong side of the law, 'tes

terrible bad *then*. Everything is against a man then; ' and the guardian of the peace went through the list again, only that this time he began with the Queen, as most remote, and ended with the policeman, as being on the spot.

" On they walked together in silence. The policeman had delivered himself of his little oration, and it had exhausted his stock of arguments on the subject.

" But meanwhile Farmer Venning's own thoughts were busy with a more solemn consideration than that of which the policeman had spoken. It had flashed in upon the farmer's mind. *This is the law of man. And if the law of man could be terrible, what about the law of God ?*

" If in spite of meaning right, a little slip that broke the law of man meant so much, what about the law of the Most High ? If to be the wrong side of man's law was to have everything against you, what when one stood on the wrong side of the law of God ? "

. . . . . .

"How the matter ended with the magistrate," said my friend, " I don't know ; I believe the magistrate took no notice of it ; but this I do know, that Farmer Venning hastened home to pour out his heart in lowly penitence before God, and there that day he did honestly and heartily accept the great salvation which is ours in Christ Jesus. He learned the truth of that blessed mystery that Christ hath redeemed us from the curse of the law, being made a curse for us, and that He is *the end of the law* for righteousness to every one that believeth.

" From that day Farmer Venning has been a power for good in all that neighbourhood; and he sometimes startles people by assuring them that *nothing ever did him so much good as the foot-and-mouth disease.*"

Where is the Bible?

THE other day I had a visit from my good friend, G. P——, a colporteur at work away on the wild Cornish coast. I should like you to know him, good reader, as a specimen of a thorough Christian worker. From a sailor who went through the Crimean War on board a saucy gunboat that was always up to some mischief, you will be sure of smartness and tact and courage. Add to this, an unflagging zeal for the Master, and a great belief and power in prayer, and you have the leading features of his character. Over moors and through valleys, for miles along that wild sea-coast, by dark "Dundagil and deep sounding Boss," lie his way and his work.

"Well, George, and what have you been doing lately?" I asked as we met.

"Hunting up Bibles, sir. And you don't know what queer places Bibles get into. I didn't know, until I began this work, and called from door to door with my books. Almost the first question I put to them is, 'Now, ma'am, have you got a Bible?' They all say, 'Yes,' and by way of getting into the house and having a talk with them, I ask to see the Book; and then I come to find out what some people do with the Bible. The good wife and mistress calls across to a shed on the other side of the little farm-yard, 'Martha!'

"Out comes the servant girl from tending the calves or the pigs, her dress turned up and a bonnet lying back loosely from her head.

"'Where's our old Bible to, Martha? Here's somebody says that he wants to see it.'

"'Don't know, mum,' says Martha; 'I haven't seen it for ever so long.'

"Turning indoors, the good mistress takes a chair,

and, standing on it, looks on the top of the dresser. There, amongst odds and ends—an old stirrup iron, a bit or two of leather, half-a-dozen old account-books—there, covered with dust, is the old Bible.

"'Dear me,' says the good woman, looking uncomfortable, 'I suppose that it was put up here when we were spring-cleaning, and the maid forgot to take it down again.'

"' Come, then, by way of making up for lost time, I think you ought to call in Martha, and I will read a chapter, and we will have a bit of prayer.' And so I get the chance of getting right at them, and bringing the Word into daylight again, for a little while at least."

"But I hope that this is only an extreme case, George. You don't often come across anything so bad as that, I suppose."

"No, not very often. The common answer is, 'O yes; I am thankful to say that we have got a lovely Bible, sir ! ' And coming into the little room, there in the window you see first a flower-pot with a geranium or lily in it, then half-a-dozen books, and under them, down at the very bottom of all, there is a large family Bible. And when the other books are taken off, they leave just four little lines of dust, ' damnation lines ' I tell them Whitefield would have called them. You see, the books have been dusted without being moved. So I can get a text out of

that—about cleaning the outside and neglecting the
heart; then I read a chapter out of the forgotten
Bible, and have a bit of prayer there too, to harrow
in the seed.

"One place I went to I found something worse
than that. When I asked the woman of the house
if she had a Bible, she shook her head very solemnly,
and said, 'Yes, she was thankful to say she had—
and a beautifuller book there wasn't in the parish,
except it was up to the parson's.' Of course, I
wanted to see this beautiful book. 'Well, she didn't
know whether I could see it, but she would bring it
down.' So, going up stairs, she brought down a large
book that was altogether stitched up in green-baize,
sewn all round, so that you couldn't get in at it anyhow at all. ''Tis such a lovely book,' said the
woman; 'I do mean that the binding of it be so
pretty, that I thought 'twas a pity for to have it
lying about for anybody to use, so I stitched it right
up. 'Twas the Squire who gave it to my boy when
his boy died—in memory of him, like."

"I took up the green-baize bundle. 'Do you
know what St. Paul told the people to pray for?'
I asked. 'It was this—"that the Word of the Lord
might have free course, and be glorified," not that it
might be bound and sewn up like this.' So I took
out my penknife and ripped it open, and then had a
talk with her about the Holy Book. Before I left

she promised me that she would read a chapter of it
every day."

When my talk with George had finished, I began
to think of where we ought to find the Bibles, and
how that one might measure the amount of religion
that people have by what they do with their Bibles.
Good reader, if my friend George had come to your
house as he came to these others, what would he find
there? Where do *you* keep the Bible, and what do
you do with it? Let me tell you

THE STORY OF THE HID TREASURE.

One day, a summer's day, a traveller walked along
the highway, parched, dusty, tired. He came to a
wayside cottage, and knocked at the door to ask for
a cup of water. The door was opened by a ragged,
slatternly woman, at whose torn skirts a lot of dirty
children clung, whilst by the open chimney sat the
sullen husband smoking his pipe.

The woman brought the traveller the water, but
the cup and the hands, and the water too, were so
dirty that he scarcely tasted it. He thanked them,
and turned to leave again, muttering to himself, yet
in a tone just loud enough for the woman to hear,
"*Ah! these people have a great treasure here if they
did but know it.*"

The woman shut the door, and turned to her husband: "Didst hear what yon man said, Dick? He

said that there was a great treasure here if we could only find it." ˷

"Why did'st not ask him where 'twas, then, stupid?" growled Dick.

"He was gone afore I could. And he didn't seem to mean me to hear it, I reckon. But if 'tis here, thou and I can find it, lad, without any of his telling?" As the woman spoke, she came to the chimney and looked at the stones, pushing one or two to see if they were loose. She had heard of people who had found old stockings full of guineas hidden in the chimney. The man's eyes followed her keenly, ready to claim the treasure if she should light upon it.

"I've heerd tell o' gould an' silver hid away under the floor. Thee'd best dig that up," grinned the man. "Thee'd find earth for certain, an' that's where the gould comed from first of all."

But no banter could shake her belief that the treasure lay there, waiting only the lucky hour for her to light upon it. As she stayed to get the children their supper, her hand stopped for a moment with the knife half-way through the round of the loaf, and her eyes went wandering over the place looking for the projecting end of the stocking. And when children and husband were in bed, she went carefully over every crack and corner, trying and prying into every hole. It grew so late

that she must give up for to-night, and off she went
to bed, but only to dream about gold pieces and piles
of silver.

Early the next morning she was at it again, and
the breakfast was more wretchedly bad than usual.
The children were neglected, the wash-tub must
wait. The wife herself looked more slatternly than
ever as the husband came home to dinner, covered
with dust as she was. He looked round at the little
cottage all in disorder, he heard the noise and
quarrelling of the children, he saw too that there
were no signs of dinner; and with a fierce curse
upon the man that had turned his wife's brain about
this treasure, he hurried away to the public-house,
and flung himself into the tap-room, more sulky and
savage even than was commonly the case with
him.

"Lass has got her head crazed about a treasure
that somebody said was in the house," Dick explained to the bustling landlady. " And if she has
got her mind on it, she'll have the house down afore
she gives in, that's the way of her. She'll die before
she'll give in."

"Eh, bless thee!" said another pot-house lounger,
dipping into the big mug of beer that he held in his
hand; "they're all aloike, she's no but a woman, an'
they never did give in, an' they never will."

"Until they meet wi' their betters," laughed the

stout old landlady, lifting her face out of the sauce-
pan from which she had been fishing the dinner;
" an' that isn't ever among you men."

Day after day of such diligent searching went on,
but without any sign of the lucky find. In vain
Dick stormed and swore, and even threatened to
proceed to further and more coercive measures.
The treasure was there, and she *would* find it; that
she would, or she would die for it. And she folded
her arms and put her lips together and nodded her
untidy head, and looked so fierce about it, that
Dick felt that he might just as well whistle against
the wind.

But slowly her hope began to fade. She had
been all over the house half-a-dozen times, and there
was not so much as a threepenny bit. Vexed at
the failure, vexed at the arrears of her work, vexed,
too, at the consequences of Dick's growing visits to
the public-house, she thought herself the one most
ill-used woman in the world. She was standing on
a rickety chair, turning over the things on the
shelf, when the chair gave way and she fell, bringing
down the shelf and all that was on it. This was the
climax of her misery. Much more hurt in mind than
in body, she kicked aside the things, and lifted the
shelf again to its uncertain rest; and then declared
aloud, "that she wouldn't bother herself any more
about it—that she wouldn't." And then she began

leisurely to pick up the things that had fallen with the shelf.

She little thought how near she was to the treasure now. The upset shelf had brought it at her feet. There it lay, right before her, and as she stooped her eyes suddenly fell upon it.

It was a book, the cover of which lay open; and looking her full in the face there was written, in an old and trembling hand, her maiden name. It was her mother's writing. The Book itself had been a gift from that mother now in heaven. Underneath the name was written this text of Scripture: "*More to be desired are they than gold, yea, than much fine gold.*"

Sitting there on the floor in her dismal cottage, in the midst of the miserable children, her thoughts began to wander back to the old mother. She saw again the little cottage, neat and clean, where she had lived. She saw, too, her own happy girlhood. She heard again that mother's cheery voice that never spoke unkindly; and the bright and happy face seemed to be looking down upon her. And here about her everything was wretched,—unkindness, dirt, misery: why was it that these crowded into her house? And why was it that they never came near her mother's cottage? All there was peace and sunshine and blessedness. Then in a moment it flashed upon her that all these good things had come to her mother *out of this Book.* And this, perhaps, was the treasure that the man had seen. Setting it carefully on the shelf again, quieted and subdued, ashamed of her own room as she kept recalling that other that had come so plainly before her, she began at once to tidy up a bit and to make the kitchen and the children and herself look a little more attractive.

Dick came home to find the supper waiting, and his wife so quiet and thoughtful that he began to think she must have found the treasure. She was a deep one, but he would be up to her if she meant to have it all to herself. He would keep a sharp lookout, said Dick to himself as he sat down to his pipe in the chimney corner. And he looked about him, trying to see if the stones had been removed.

That night, when all was quiet, when the husband and children were safe in bed, the wife stayed to take down the treasure and to read again its old familiar pages. But it was another book now. The mother's face looked at her from every page ; and with strange distinctness the mother's voice seemed to be reading the words. And bowing down in earnest prayer, she besought the mercy of her mother's God, and confessed her wicked forgetfulness of Him. In her troubled sleep that face haunted her still, and the voice called her. She woke, and again in the darkness lifted up her heart for mercy, and promised once more, by God's help, that she would live to Him, and diligently seek the way to heaven.

Day after day passed, leaving Dick more and more astonished at the change that had come over his wife. Her very appearance and manner were altered. There was a cleanliness about her now that spread to the children and to the cottage. "There," said Dick to himself, "plain enough she has found the treasure, and she isn't so much as going halves." . His suspicions were confirmed by another circumstance. It was plain that his wife had something on her mind. She was wonderfully quiet for one thing, and when she did speak, spoke sadly and gently, as if some trouble pressed upon her. She often went away upstairs by herself, and very often sighed. And when Dick asked her what was amiss, she only looked out of the window, and said that she would tell him some day. Dick fancied she brushed away a tear, and having no sympathy with any such weakness, he only grunted a savage "Umph," and smoked his pipe. "I'll find thee out, my lass; and if thee have spent it all, then thee'lt smart," he muttered to himself, puffing away angrily.

The opportunity thus watched for soon arrived. Dick noticed that early each morning, before anybody else was stirring, his wife was dressed and went downstairs; noticed, too, that she was very quiet down there, as if she were afraid to let anybody know

M

what she was doing. Now putting it all together, Dick had no doubt that if he could but come upon her there, "the murder would out," as he said.

Giving her time to get well at the mystery, whatever it might be, he rose very quietly, and then crept to the stairs, from which he could see at once into the kitchen below. There, with her back towards him, knelt the wife, and the opened Book before her.

"'Tis bank-notes, of course," said Dick, proud at the discovery, "and to think of hiding 'em in that old Book! I've got her now." And wondering how much it might be, and with golden visions dancing before him, he completed his dressing. By the time he was downstairs the good wife was attending to the children; so, creeping stealthily to the Bible, he took it, and shook it with the leaves turned downward, so that the contents might fall out. But no notes came fluttering to the floor.

"Ah! pinned in, I s'pose," said Dick, slightly disappointed. He turned to the cover, and then looked at page after page. But there was nothing. "Too late ; she has cleared 'em all. But I'll be up to her."

Dick spent the day revolving some other method of getting at the secret. As he came home at the end of the day's work, the brightness of the cottage, the cheerfulness of the children, the pleasant greeting of his wife, impressed him more than ever, and raised an ugly fear that the money must be going rather freely. "He would keep his eyes open, and if he didn't find out that evening, he *would* get it out of her somehow;" and surly Dick lit his pipe, and puffed fiercely.

But that night it came out. The children were in bed, and all was quiet, when the wife sat down by Dick's side with her work. For some time she sat in silence, Dick watching her curiously, and owning to himself that, after all, his lass could hold her own with any of them, when she made the best of herself. Then she looked up suddenly :

"Dick, lad, I've got something to tell thee, and I'm very much mistaken if it isn't the treasure that I've found."

"Come, lass, I was thinking so much; and I thought thee would never be so mean as to keep it all to thysel'," replied Dick, greatly relieved.

"I don't want to, Dick, I'm sure," said his wife tenderly.

"And thee may be just so sure that I shan't say thee nay in that matter, lass," laughed Dick. "Is it gold or silver, much or little ? "

But whilst Dick was speaking, she was standing at the shelf, and brought down the old Book.

" Thee wert very warm, then, after all," he thought to himself. " The right place, but thine eyes weren't sharp enough. Eh, but the women are deep ! "

M 2

"I believe that this is what the man meant, Dick." And she turned to the fly-leaf. "Look at what it says here: '*More to be desired are they than gold, yea, than much fine gold.*' My mother gave me this Bible, and wrote that, Dick; and I know what a treasure she found it, for this life and for the next too."

Dick sank back disappointed. No bank notes, no gold, not even a crock of shillings. After all, nothing but an old Book. But his wife was a deep one, as Dick said, and went on quietly:

"Now, Dick, I'll tell thee what I've been thinking,—that if this Book can make me so good a wife to thee, dear lad, and so good a mother to thy bairns, and thy home so pleasant, as it made my mother and my home years ago, it really will be better than gold. Now look, Dick, I'm going to try it, and I think that thou couldst do much worse than take thy share o' the treasure, and try it with me."

As the wife spoke, she had laid down the work, and her hand rested on Dick's. Now she looked at him with the earnest eyes and spoke with the tenderness of old times: "Thee hast had enough to put up with in me, lad, and I'm sorry for it; but, by God's help, I'll be to thee what I never have been yet. I'm beginning to see things different already."

Dick didn't quite know what to make of all this. A man of few words and slow thought, he felt bewildered, and sat looking in at the fire, turning matters over for some time before he could quite take it all in. The wife was hurrying on with her work ; as he turned he caught sight of her as she sat beside him, looking just like she used to in those courting days ten years ago. He looked around, too, at the little place, already so much brighter and cheerier. The very cat that rubbed itself against his wife's chair had taken to purr more loudly than it ever had done before ; and if all *that* was to come out of the treasure, Dick wasn't going to lose his share in it.

"There, lass, there's my hand for thee. I'll be halves in thy treasure."

That night Dick and his wife read their first chapter together from the mother's Bible, and then he kneeled beside his wife, joining in her simple, earnest prayer to her mother's God.

. . . . . .

Now, good reader, where is your Bible, and *what are you doing with it ?* It is not enough to have one in the house, or a score, for that matter. *Have your own.* Get used to handling it, and to know your way through it. Let no day pass without finding something in God's Word to turn over in your thoughts during the day. Here search

diligently like the wise men did of old, and you shall
find the Lord Jesus. Here turn with prayer and
earnest seeking, and you shall find a Guide for every
way, a Comfort for every sorrow, a Balm for every
fear, a Cure for all troubles, and a Hope that shall
shine always. It is the plain command of our
heavenly Master, as much for us as for them of old
time, " SEARCH THE SCRIPTURES, FOR THESE ARE
THEY WHICH TESTIFY OF ME."

How Mark Neighbour held His Own.

THE scene was peaceful enough, and nothing about it suggested the battle-field. Mark Neighbour was by no means a fighting man, but a carpenter, who had risen first to be the foreman of the workshop, and then to have the place and business for his own. Now that, to begin with, is a peaceful kind of a business, and, except in the matter of the gallows, is chiefly concerned with the comforts of life, and has but little to do with its conflicts.

It was the dinner-hour now, and they sat together in the sunshine, the men resting on the bits of timber that lay in the place. The shavings and sawdust gave a pleasant pine odour. The sunshine slanted in at the open door and fell in great splats of golden light on the bench, and gleamed on the turning-lathe, and shone on the tools; and reached far enough across to touch the opposite side and illuminate the lower part of a *British Workman* wall-picture that was set up there, adorned with a frame of red braid, and fastened at the corners with orna-mental nails. The picture seemed to greet everybody that came in with a kind of welcome, and modestly proclaimed the principles of the man who owned the place.

It was Blinks who was speaking. "Blinks" he was always called, although the rest were known by their Christian names. Blinks was a kind of man that you never got to know well enough to find out if he had any other name.

"Well, what I say is this," said Blinks, "to sign a pledge is no better than slavery. Sign a pledge! Why, it's like as if a fellow was a baby, and couldn't trust hisself to take care of hisself."

"And sure it's a deal you know about babies, Blinks," laughed Tim Reilly; for Blinks was a bachelor, and looked it, every inch of him—a long-faced, sallow-coloured man, with a stubbly beard of a week's growth, that never seemed to get more or less. On either side of his face ran deep lines of discontent, and his lips were fixed into a scorn at things in general. Any judge of timber could tell that if you were to saw through Blinks, you would find him a very cross-grained piece, and full of knots.

He took no notice of Tim's remark, but held his short black pipe in his hand, whilst he had his say :—

"What I say is this : that a man isn't fit to be a man, and to be trusted with liberty, if he goes sign-ing it away and making a slave of hisself. Why'

" Whatever is it ? " says mother.

[See p. 183.

he might as well shut hisself up in a dungeon for
fear the light of day might hurt him, and never
come out at night for fear the midges would bite
him. A man hasn't got any right to go doing away
with the right to please hisself—and putting it down
on a piece of paper that he won't drink. Bah!"

And Blinks drew fiercely at his pipe—partly
because it was nearly out, but mostly because it was
a relief to his indignation—and he blew it off in
short, sharp clouds of smoke.

"Well," said Mark, "if a man is to have the right
to please himself, why shouldn't he be able to please
himself in signing the pledge, as well as in anything
else ? And as for being a slave—well, there's worse
things than being a slave."

"There's bein' a master, for instance," said Tim,
slyly.

"Yes, there's being a master," said Mark, joining
in the laugh at his own expense. "But I was going
to say it all depends what anybody is a slave to.
The greatest thing in the world is to be a slave like
one I read about in the book"—and Mark drew out
his New Testament—"who took upon Him the form
of a servant. And a finer man never lived than one
I have read about here, who called himself the slave
of Jesus Christ. Why, bless me, a man is not a
man at all, only a thing like my little Mark makes
when he gets hold of a bit of putty—pulled into

arms and legs, with a big dab for a body, and a little
dab for a head—unless there's scores of things that
he dare not please himself about. A man can't anyhow keep upright, but will fall all to pieces unless
he has got a big *I must* running right down through
him like an iron pillar. I can't please myself about
the thing that is fair and honest. A man *must* keep
his hands from picking and stealing, or else down
comes the law with a pair of handcuffs and the
inside of a dungeon like Blinks told about, and
makes a slave of him in quick time. I've got to be
a slave to keep the law or to suffer for it—one or the
other. But there's thousands of things about which
I can't please myself, because I *am* a man and not a
baby. Bless you, Blinks, for all your talk, I'd just
like to see you if a house was on fire, and up at the
window a little one was standing shrieking for help.
Please yourself! not a bit! For all your talk you
know well enough you would first have that little
one out, or you would be trying to, and nobody would
say Blinks wasn't a man for doing it. It's the finest
thing in the world for a man to be a slave if he is
only a slave to the right thing. And now, lads, I'll
put it to you honestly. Which is the best thing?
To be a slave to the drink—a slave to the thing
that steals a man's senses, and wastes his money,
and sends him home to be a curse to his wife and
children; a slave to a thing that leaves him a fool

to-night, and makes him a miserable fellow to-morrow, until he has had a glass or two to pull him together a bit—that's to be a slave if you like, and there's no running away from that master in a hurry. Isn't it a better thing to say, 'No, I can't please myself about a thing that makes so much mischief, and I'll sign a pledge that I won't touch it so long as I live'? And he makes a slave of himself that he may keep his head clear and his hands steady, and his home happy, and his children well-fed and well-clothed, and his soul sweet, and his mind right—that's a right good kind of slavery, that is. No, my lads, it's the finest thing in the world to be a slave to the right thing. To do right things and think right thoughts till a man is just a slave to it, and can't please himself, is about the best liberty that I can think of in this world or any other."

"That's right enough," said Jack Norris as if it were a kind of sermon to be agreed with, chiefly because it was done. "But after all, what Blinks says has got a good deal in it. What in the world does a man want to sign the pledge for? Surely if he wants to do a thing he can do it without that. It does seem silly to go sticking your name down upon a piece of paper."

Mark was rather slow in replying. After putting up at a station, it took him some time to start and get into full speed again.

"Well," he began, stooping to pick up a shaving and curling it round his finger, "I can't see that, Jack. All I know is that I have signed the pledge three times, and you may take any one of those three pledges and you won't find anything very silly in either of them. If I had my time to go over again, I would ask for nothing better than to sign those three pledges."

"*Three*—how do you make that out?" grunted Blinks, without removing his pipe this time.

Mark's face spread into smiles and his eyes twinkled as he said, "Well, you see, Blinks, the first pledge that I signed came about in this way. I met a pretty young girl one day, and I asked her to be my wife. It was a happy day for me, I can tell you, when she said she would; but that wasn't such a happy day as when I signed the pledge."

"Come, come," said Tim, "it's a good thing she isn't here."

"Well, we were married, we two, and I never did a better day's work than that. And then I signed the pledge."

"What pledge?" It was a grunt that came from Blinks, and was followed by a big puff of smoke.

"Why, the pledge that I would love her and cherish her so long as I lived—as pretty a pledge, to my mind, as ever came to mortal lips when two hearts say it together. I wish you knew how pretty it is, Blinks; it would be the making of you. Yes, I put my name down in black and white, and had it witnessed and all. I signed my liberty away—couldn't please myself by marrying anybody else so long as we lived, and I never wished my liberty back again, and I don't think I ever shall. Now, Jack, I don't see anything like making a fool of myself in that."

Blinks took his pipe out of his mouth and blew a longer, bigger cloud of indignation than ever. " Bah," he growled.

But Tim Reilly laughed, " Sure and Blinks would like to sign that pledge if he could, only it takes two to do it, and the other is hard to find with some folks."

Blinks puffed in scornful silence.

" Well," Mark went on, " the next pledge was number two; and all I can say is that I shouldn't mind signing a pledge like that once a year for the next thirty years. And I reckon Tim Reilly would like to sign that as well, and Blinks and the rest of us. Bless you, it *was* a pledge, stiff and solemn and all full of ' the aforesaid' and the rest of it. There was a big stamp upon it and half a dozen seals at the bottom of it. I had to sign my name, but I didn't think it very silly sticking my name on the thing, and putting my finger on the seal to declare that it was

my act and deed. The lawyer's clerk had to witness
it. A solemn sort of a thing it seemed to be, with all
the signings and witnessings, but there was nothing
babyish about it, I can tell you. I put my name in
a big round hand, MARK NEIGHBOUR. Babyish! not
a bit of it! When I had done it I felt like a lord,
and held my head that high that the missus saw
there was something up and asked me right off,
before I could say a word, what it was all about.
So I told her that I had *bought a house all for her
own*, and that we were going to live in it, and that it
was paid for, too. And I took out a big blue enve-
lope with the parchment in it, and she tried to read
it through, but never got further than the third
line, for her eye skips down to see my name at the
bottom. She wanted to have it framed and hung up
in the parlour of the new house, for she said that
she couldn't think of a prettier picture to put up on
the wall. Well, away we went that day, and I
began to trim the roses about the porch and the
wife began to clean the windows and to put up
the blinds. She said that she didn't envy the
Queen now that she had got a house of her own
to live in. That is a good kind of pledge to sign,
my lads, and I wish you could every one of you
go sticking your name to a thing like that. What
do you say to that, Blinks! There's nothing babyish
about that, is there?"

Blinks smoked in silence, since even he could not grunt at that.

"Well, then there was pledge number three, and I put my name to that. I didn't feel that any sillier than the other two. I shouldn't have had much of the man about me if I could have done anything else.

"It is seventeen years ago, and we were living a good way from here. And Elsie was just seven, and a handy little thing she was too, looking after the little ones and doing all sorts of things for mother—her 'right hand,' mother called her. Every day at dinner and supper she used to fetch the beer, taking the jug and the money down to the public-house at the corner of the street. Well, one night she had gone, but she was a long time coming back, so presently we began to be a bit anxious, and I put on my hat and went out, wondering what in the world had happened and fearing all sorts of things.

"When I got to the public-house door there was a crowd of people round it, and I found there was a drunken row going on. A fellow had been fighting and had hit the barman on the head with a pewter pot, and cut it open. The blood was streaming down his face, covering him. There was the policeman and a half a dozen of them trying to lay hold of the fellow, he kicking and biting like a

N

madman. A couple of half-drunk women were
with him and took up the quarrel, scratching and
screaming and using all the foulest language that
they could think of. And there, white as a sheet,
with the tears streaming down her cheeks, trembling
from head to foot, was little Elsie.

"I pushed my way through them all, and caught
her up in my arms. She laid her head against me
and sobbed in her fright, clinging to me, and starting
at every blow and shriek.

"I managed to get safely out of the place, but it
was a long time before she got over her fright, sobbing and trembling for an hour or more. At last
we got her to bed and she was soon asleep, but I
suppose she began dreaming of the man with the
gash in his head. Anyhow, she woke up with a
scream, and when I came upstairs she sat there
sobbing, and trembling from head to foot. I took
her on my knee, and sat down by the fire with my
arm about her, the poor little thing so pale and
frightened, I could hardly bear to see her. Then
she dropped asleep again, and in her sleep there came
a long quivering breath and then a great sob that
went through me. The wife was leaning over my
shoulder, putting back the little one's curls a bit
from her face.

"'Mother,' I said, 'what a fool I was ever to let
her go to such a place as that—to think of her see-

ing a sight like that of to-night, and hearing words
like those, which shouldn't have come near her for a
hundred pounds if I could have helped it. Help it !
I will for the future, anyhow—and no child of mine
shall ever go to fetch my beer again as long as I
live, if I have to go without a glass of beer to my
dying day ! '

" Then the little one woke up, and putting her arm
about my neck, she said, ' Father, I am so sorry,
you have not had your supper beer to-night.'

"'I stooped and kissed the little white face, and
there and then I vowed that I would never touch the
stuff again. So mother and Elsie and me, we signed
the pledge together. And a better man I've been
for it ever since.

" There, lads, that's three pledges that I signed,
and I can't see anything silly in any one of them,
and I don't know of anything much better for
everybody living."

It really seemed as if there was nothing more to
be said, when suddenly the silence was broken by
'Lisha Widgery, a west country youth with a
squeaky voice,—

" They do tell me that teetotalism do make anybody feel so weak and frail. What do yew
think ? "

Certainly the objection could not have come from
anybody with such little fitness as from 'Lisha, a

long, overgrown, loose-limbed lad, who always looked
as if he wanted screwing up: his small head pro-
jected as if even its weight were too much for the
shoulders. He blushed when he spoke, and seemed
to make the remark by way of showing what a strong
man he must be.

Then it was that Mark Neighbour called up his
reserve. " Well, Martin, what do you say to that ? "
And then he turned to 'Lisha, " Martin Chubb has
tried both sides, so he ought to know."

Martin was a thick-set man, with his hands pushed
deep in his pockets ; one leg was thrust under him
and the other thrust out, while he seemed to be playing hide-and-seek with his toe—putting his head on
one side always exactly opposite to that towards
which he turned his foot. But being called upon
thus suddenly, Martin was scarcely ready for action.
He never rushed into the battle "like the unthink-
ing horse " of which one used to hear. He started,
and thrust his hand up to his head and began rub-
bing it mightily, as if to gather his wits together.
Then came a chuckle, a deep chuckle that shook his
waistcoat —" *That is a good un, that is.*"

And the chuckle came again. It was an internal
chuckle that scarcely spread a ripple on his face. It
came up every now and then like a big bubble rises
sometimes in still water and breaks on the surface—
" *That is a good un.*"

You would have thought that this was all Martin had to say on the subject, but another chuckle woke him up, and, putting his hands back into his pockets and balancing head and foot, he began,—

"Weak! Make anybody weak! Well, I ought to know. When I was a drinking chap, which I was up to four year agone, I was weak if you like, weaker than a child. Bless you, I was that weak I couldn't carry so much as a threepenny-bit past a public-house—not to save my head. Weak! No, I couldn't lift my foot to go so much as a yard further, not if twenty mad bulls had been coming after me."

Then came the pause, and the chuckle slowly worked its way up and reached the surface,—"Well, that is a good one, that is." That to himself; then to the company in general he continued his story :—"I was saying I was weak, but weak isn't the word for it. Well, I turned teetotal and signed the pledge. I got a money-box and kept it always handy, and whenever I feeled like having a drink I puts in a threepenny-bit. I kept a few handy, for I used to feel like having a drink eight or nine times a day at the first going off, besides the regular allowance at meal-times. Well, they keeped dropping in, did they threepennies until the box began to get a bit heavyish—it was wonderful how they keeped coming on. You see, whenever I met an old pal I should shift a threepenny aside for the box; and when I met two or three of 'em 'pon a Saturday night, I used to think I let myself off uncommon easy for four threepennies—I might a-made it eight without cheating myself."

He paused whilst another chuckle found its escape—" That is a good un, that is."

" Well, may be I had signed teetotal nine months, may be a little over—it was in the spring of the year, I can mind that. I had been down to see the old mother, and it was a Friday night. She'd been a-washing all the week, so she says, ' Martin,' says she, ' come here, my dear, will you, and tie up my wrists, they're bleeding ? '

" ' What's that along with, mother ? ' I says, for they was all chapped dreadful.

" ' Why, along with the washing,' says she. ' You see these here cold east winds is bad, and the rough towels, wringing them out is sure to chap your wrists to pieces.'

" ' Well, I didn't say nothing to nobody, but I up and straight away home. I got hold of that box and turned out the money. Eh, but it was a pile of threepennies ! I didn't think there was so many threepennies in the world. I never said a word to anybody, but off I goes, and into a shop where they sells they wringing-machines. So I picked one out that I thought was the very thing and asks the man, How much ?

" ' Do you mind having it in threepennies ? ' says I.

" ' Not a bit,' says he, ' so long as I get it some-how.'

" So I out with the bag and plumps it down. And he counts them up in little piles, and that job was done.

" ' Where shall I send it ? ' says he, quite perlite.

" ' Nowheres,' says I, ' for I'll carry it myself.'

" 'Carry it ?' says he ; ' you can't, it will break your back.'

" ' Can't I ? ' says I. ' Bless ye, I'm teetotal, I am, and can carry anything.'

" It *was* a stiffish load, that I will say. But I did it, I really did. I, Martin Chubb, a man who couldn't carry a threepenny-bit past a public-house for my life, carried that thing past a score of public-houses, and never stopped till I come to old mother's house.

" ' Whatever is it ? ' says mother, hearing some-body staggering about the door and banging in to the passage.

" ' All right, mother,' I says ; ' there's no call for to be frightened,' and I plumps it down.

" ' Is it a barrel-organ ? ' says mother.

" ' No, mother,' says I, ' it ain't. It is a cure for chapped wrists.'

" ' A what ? ' says she.

" So I showed her what it was, and I showed her

how to use it. Dear old mother. Says she, 'But, Martin,' says she, ''tis come by honest, ain't it, or it would be worse than chapped wrists?'

"Honest! Bless you, mother, I've a-turned tee-total and put the money into a wringing-machine, and here it is, your very own."

"Mother, she comes and puts her arm about me, and says she, 'Turned teetotal! Well, Martin, I never knowed you had much sense,' says she, 'but if you've turned teetotal you've a-got more sense in your little finger than the rest of 'em have a-got in their whole body. And I'm proud of you, Martin,' says she, 'if I never was before,' says she."

The dinner-hour was over and the company broke up, but there came a final chuckle from Martin Chubb—"Well! well, that was a good un, that was."

HAYMAN, CHRISTY, & LILLY, LTD., Printers, 113, Farringdon Rd., E. C